All about the Rottweiler

Leo von Oversticht
– a dog from the
early days of the
breed – born
3 February 1911.

All about the Rottweiler

MARY MACPHAIL

PELHAM BOOKS

First published in Great Britain by
Pelham Books Ltd
44 Bedford Square
London WC1B 3DP
1986

British Library Cataloguing in Publication Data

Macphail, Mary
   All about the Rottweiler.
   1. Rottweiler dog.
   I. Title
   636.7′3   SF429.R7

ISBN 0-7207-1600-4

Typeset, printed and bound by
Butler & Tanner Ltd, Frome and London

Contents

Acknowledgements

I am most grateful to those who kindly helped with suggestions and information for this book, in particular:

General advice – Kay White. Reading the drafts of various chapters and offering constructive suggestions – Joan Blackmore, Elizabeth Harrap, Roy Hunter, Jane Trowbridge and Joan Wheatcroft. Additional veterinary information – R. A. Cathcart BSc, MRCVS, Layton Animal Hospital; D. G. Clayton-Jones MRCVS, DVR, The Royal Veterinary College; D. G. Lewis FRCVS, DVR, Small Animal Hospital, University of Liverpool. Information on the breed overseas – Aage Christensen, Denmark; Elina Haapaniemi, Finland; Sonia Feldmann, Norway; Pat and Maxine Kauri, New Zealand; Gunvor af Klinteberg-Jarvarud, Sweden; Colonel Pettengell, Australia; Dov Rosental, Israel; Gwen Watley, Trinidad; K. K. Yeo, Malaysia.

My thanks also are due to the many people who sent in photographs; it was far from easy to choose and many excellent ones had to be left out.

Mary Macphail
Hampshire, 1985

PHOTO CREDITS

The author and publishers are grateful to the following for permission to reproduce copyright photographs in this book: Liz Brendon page *43*; Dick Delany *59, 60, 61, 77, 81*; P. Diment *24*; Gunther Feldmann *50, 62, 74, 88, 105, 117, 130*; Fox Photos *18*; Gerald Foyle *25*; E. R. Hellemaa *133*; J. Holland *32*; G. B. Ogilvy Shepherd *107*; Diane Pearce *26, 115* (top); Anne Roslin-Williams *115* (bottom); M. St Maur Sheil *42*; Sally Anne Thompson *28*. In some cases it has not been possible to ascertain the copyright holder and it is hoped that any such omissions will be excused.

1 Origins

The Beginnings

Speculation on the immediate forebears of the dog as well as the time and place of domestication has occupied the talents of cynologists and naturalists for many years, and the available evidence is open to a range of interpretations.

According to Scott (1963), three main theories have been proposed to account for the origin of the dog: that it was domesticated from a wild species which later became extinct (Allan 1920); that it was evolved from at least two species, the wolf and the golden jackal, to account for the great inter- and intra-breed variation (Darwin 1859); and that it was domesticated from a local variety of small wolf. It is the last theory which is generally regarded as the most likely.

To determine relationships with other varieties, comparisons have been made between anatomical features. Differences have been found to be mainly a tooth characteristic. In the large northern wolves, the teeth are large in relation to the skull, but in the smaller Indian wolf the size of the tooth resembles that of dogs with a similar sized skull (Lawrence 1967). Comparative studies of chromosomes have also been done with a very small sample, and these have shown that all members of the genus *Canis* have a diploid chromosome number – 78. However most research has concentrated on studies of the behavioural patterns of dogs and wolves, and from these it has been found that there is a close resemblance in all behavioural patterns in both species. Very few patterns have not been observed in both which supports the hypothesis that a close relationship does exist. Despite the fact that similar detailed research has not yet been carried out with the coyote and jackal, there is some evidence that they are different from dogs and wolves. Indeed, one of the prominent traits of wolves and dogs is that they possess a highly social nature. In the wild, wolves hunt in packs but jackals and coyotes do not – their typical group consists of a mated pair and a litter. Vocalisations also differ, with wolves and dogs showing the same pattern of barking and howling, whilst jackals and coyotes have a much more varied repertoire.

Domestication

Present research indicates that dogs have been domesticated for at least 10,000 years and possibly longer. The oldest known dog remains which have definitely been identified were found in the Beaverhead Mountains, Idaho, USA, and carbon dating methods place this specimen at the latest 8400 BC and at the earliest 9500 BC.

Throughout the world prehistoric man was surrounded by wild dogs. Both were hunters, and dogs in addition, were scavengers. The theory that an association between dogs and man began on the basis of a hunting partnership has not received universal acceptance. Zeuner (1963) postulates instead that it was based on scavenging: man appreciated the usefulness of having scavengers to remove food debris from his camps and so tolerated the presence of wild dogs. The social propensities of dogs and wolves are well known, and it is well documented how easily wolves are tamed when young, so it would not have been difficult for primitive man to begin an association with them and to perceive the varied uses, apart from scavenging, to which dogs could be put – hunting, herding, guarding and, later, as pets and companions.

The increasing use of the dog for other purposes took place over thousands of years, and during this time many new varieties appeared, some of which can be identified with breeds existing today while others, for one reason or another, have disappeared or become so diluted with other blood that they are changed beyond recognition. With the acquisition of new skills in cultivation, the resulting increased population, greater specialisation of labour and a more settled way of life, hunting, hitherto a necessity for survival, became a sport for which different varieties of dogs were used. A large mastiff-like dog was used for hunting large animals such as lions and wild horses, and smaller gaze hounds were used for coursing animals like the hare and deer. Very large breeds were also used for protection and in war.

The Development of Breeds

Fiennes and Fiennes (1968) suggest that modern dogs may be classified under four main headings according to origin, all deriving from different types of wolves.
1. Dingo group from the Asian wolf.
2. Northern group (including Spitz breeds, German Shepherd dogs and Terriers) from the northern wolf.
3. Greyhound group from a cursorial wolf ancestor.
4. Mastiff group from mountain wolves.
This fourth group, with which we are concerned, shows the most diversity which lends support to the hypothesis that several ancestors rather than just one were involved. Despite the great variation in

form, size and colour, there are characteristics common to most breeds: good scenting ability, a head which possesses a pronounced stop, pendant ears, short or very short muzzles and a fine, often silky coat.

This group includes mastiffs, bulldogs and related breeds, scent hounds, gundog types and small dogs of pug or pekinese type. The area of origin of all these breeds is thought to be the great ridge of mountains stretching from the Himalayas in the east to the Alps and Pyrenees in the west. Mastiffs were probably the first breed to guard the flocks, a task which needed resolution, strength and speed. These qualities led to their use in war and for hunting – large Molossian mastiffs accompanied the all-conquering Roman legions. Three types of herding dog were used by the Romans; the Molossos, the wolf-like sheepdog and the short-haired herding dog, which they brought with them over the Alps as it was then necessary to drive cattle with the armies in order to ensure adequate supplies. There then took place a mixing of these Roman dogs with native varieties from which evolved the ancestors of the Rottweiler. As Korn wrote, 'There developed in the area of the Rhine and its side valleys ... a special breed of dog which one may describe as the fortunate result of the mingling of the best physical and mental qualities of Roman fighting dogs, native cattle dogs and broad-mouthed forms of British and Dutch bulldogs. ... From the little town of Rottweil, a former Roman colony, it received in the Middle Ages the name, Rottweil Butcher's dog ...'.

The German Background

Today, the idea of a Rottweiler being any colour other than black with tan markings is unlikely to enter the minds of those interested in the breed, but this smart colour scheme and robust balanced appearance were very different in the early dogs. The first standard, that issued by the International Club for Leonberger and Rottweiler Dogs in 1901, stated that although black with rust or yellow markings was the preferred colour, variations were permitted: 'black stripes on an ash gray background with yellow markings, plain red with black nose, dark wolf gray with black head and saddle but always with yellow markings'. White markings on the chest and legs occurred very frequently and were permitted provided that they were not too extensive.

Nowadays, for any breed of dog to flourish in the western world, it is necessary that a breed organisation be formed to protect its interests, agree on a standard and, in the case of countries where registration of stock is not carried out by a central agency, to maintain a breed register.

A typical German Rottweiler imported into the USA, Ch. Berit v. Alemannenhof. Owned by Clara Hurley and Michael Grossman.

Before the formation of any club, the future of the Rottweiler had looked bleak. He had been employed in the task of driving cattle long distances to market, guarding them and driving off wolves and rustlers, but the advent of the railways deprived him of this work as it was then forbidden by law for dogs to carry out the work. Then he found another occupation as a butcher's dog, pulling little carts, but here again he was superseded when the donkey was introduced as a

PEDIGREE OF
CH. BERIT VOM ALEMANNENHOF

PARENTS	GRANDPARENTS	GREAT-GRANDPARENTS	GREAT-GREAT-GRANDPARENTS
Kai v Tengen/III HD Free	Dago v Hause Normann/III HD Free	Dack v d Meierei/III HD Free	Alex v Kloster Disibodenberg/II HD +
	Anja v Silberwald HD Free	Anja v Silberwald HD Free	Barbel v Grevingsberg/I HD Free
		Bulli v Hungerbuhl/II HD Free	Brutus v Georgshof/III HD Free
	Etzel v St Andreasberg/III HD Free	Cora v Jakobsbrunnen/III	Jessy v d Hobertsburg/I
			Kuno v Butzensee/III
		Berno v Albtal/III HD Free	Britta v Schlossberg
			Emir v Durrbach/I
Hanna v Hause Normann/I HD Free	Conni v Silberwald/I HD Free	Anne v Bauerngraben/III HD Free	Sella v Jakobsbrunnen/II
			Hasso v Oelberg/III HD Free
			Heidi v Durrbach
		Dack v d Meierei/III HD Free	Alf v Schnellbahn/I
			Anja v d Kaltenweide/I
		Jessy v d Hobertsburg/I	Alex v Kloster Disibodenberg/II HD +
			Barbel v Grevingsberg/I HD Free
			Emir v Freienhagen/III HD +
			Nelli v Silahopp/I HD Free

draught animal. So for a while the Rottweiler was without a job, and numbers declined considerably; at the turn of the century there was only one bitch to be found in the town of Rottweil. However the future of the breed was assured when it became recognised as a working dog in 1910, joining the German Shepherd, Dobermann and Airedale.

The International Club for Leonberger and Rottweiler Dogs was established in 1899, but it was short-lived and, apart from publishing the first breed standard, made no significant contribution. The German Rottweiler Club (DRK) was formed in January 1907 and the South German Rottweiler Club (SDRK) came into being in April of the same year due to internal friction in the DRK, followed soon after by the International Rottweiler Club which took over from the fading SDRK. Yet another South German Club was formed in 1919 but soon disappeared from view. Eventually in 1921 the two remaining clubs were united to form the General German Rottweiler Club (ADRK) which remains to this day the sole organisation in the homeland of the Rottweiler responsible for all matters pertaining to the breed. These include the registration of litters, the issuing of pedigrees, conducting tests of suitability for breeding, training and approval both of breed and working trials judges, maintaining and publishing the breed books issued at regular intervals as well as implementing the breed warden system, conformation shows and working trials.

With the unification of the two clubs, planned breeding to improve the external appearance of the Rottweiler continued, and in 1923 a regulation was introduced that only black and tan Rottweilers would be registered in the breed book and receive pedigrees. Two further regulations came into force: to be eligible for registration, both parents must already be registered and have been at least eighteen months old at the time of mating; and not more than eight puppies in a litter could be registered. Later, long-coated specimens were excluded from breeding. Great strides were made in producing a more refined and harmonious animal and these changes will be discussed further in Chapter 3.

Functions of the German Rottweiler Club (ADRK)

Germany is a country which belongs to the Federation Cynologique Internationale, a central organisation located in Brussels to whose regulations the national kennel clubs of most countries (excluding USA, Canada, England, Australia and New Zealand) are subject. Although there is a national Kennel Club in Germany, it differs considerably from our own in that it is not the central body for registrations of all breeds, but it does select show dates for all-breed shows. Grass roots administration is left in the hands of the breed clubs, and it is impossible to overestimate their importance.

By our standards, the German Rottweiler Club is a very complex organisation, necessarily so because of its multi-faceted role: approving kennel affixes, registration of puppies, issuing pedigrees, instituting and monitoring tests of suitability for breeding (Zuchttauglichkeitsprüfung) and the Selection (Körung), recording results of all shows and trials, ensuring the maintenance of quality in the breed through the breed warden system and by the training and approval of conformation and performance judges, and responsibility for area groups.

The ADRK issues a booklet which is a most comprehensive publication giving precise regulations for breeding, definition of systems, e.g. inbreeding, line-breeding, outcrossing; maximum ages for dog (nine years) and bitch (eight years); minimum age for both (24 months); frequency of breeding (not more than once a year); functions of breed wardens; rules for tests of suitability for breeding and 'selection' etc. The ADRK also produces the stud book which lists all litters born, giving name and number allocated to each puppy, working qualifications of parents and grandparents, results of tests of suitability for breeding and selection, together with a report on each dog/bitch, results of working trials, list of dogs/bitches which have been X-rayed (hips) with results, lists of dogs/bitches which are considered unsuitable for breeding with reason(s), for example missing teeth, entropion/ectropion, hip status not sufficiently good, incorrect temperament, etc.

The stud book is published every year or two, so there is a continuous record of animals used for breeding, and since detailed critiques are given on each, this is an invaluable source of information for breeders and those seeking foundation stock, both from Germany and foreign countries.

The major difference between breeding operations in Germany and in this country (and others such as the USA, Canada, Australia, New Zealand, etc) is that puppies will be registered by the German Club only if both parents have passed the test of suitability for breeding. Furthermore, there are restrictions, as mentioned above, on the age at which stock may be used for breeding. As well as legislating that bitches may not have more than one litter a year, dogs must not mate more than two bitches a week and not more than forty in one year. I am in total agreement with these requirements. Breeders are permitted to choose the breeding partners for their dogs and bitches, but are recommended to seek the advice of the area breed warden.

Breed wardens (and occasionally judges of the breed) officiate at this breeding test at which the dog's body measurements are recorded and reports written on its conformation and movement as well as various aspects of its character including protective and guarding instincts. Apart from the basic test of suitability for breeding, top quality dogs and bitches may be entered for the highest test of breeding suitability, the selection or Körung. To be eligible for this, there is a minimum working qualification, for bitches SchH1, for dogs SchH3; animals must be HD-free or have borderline hips; have received gradings in the show ring of Excellent or Very Good under different judges; and their progeny must not have shown any serious genetic faults such as long coats, poor temperaments, high proportion of hip dysplasia, etc. These criteria are changed from time to time but the essentials remain the same. Those dogs/bitches of superior merit which pass the Körung are 'endorsed' (their pedigrees marked 'gekört') and must be re-presented for the test after two years. If they (and their progeny) still fulfil the stiff requirements laid down, they are considered to be 'endorsed' for life (marked gekört EzA). Not many dogs achieve this status and their progeny are in great demand.

The Show Scene
Once again, there is a vast difference between shows in this country and in Germany where dogs are entered in one class only, are graded by the judge as Excellent (V), Very Good (SG), Good (G), Satisfactory (Gd), or Unsatisfactory (M). The judge writes a report on their conformation and movement, a copy of which is given to the exhibitor at the conclusion of the class and another is retained by the Club.

Classes, scheduled on an age basis are usually 9–12 months, 12–18 months, 18–24 months, 2 years and over without working qualification, 2 years and over with working qualification. The sexes are always judged separately. The highest grading given in the first two classes is Very Good and in the third class only dogs/bitches of perfect conformation are awarded an Excellent grading and there must be a good entry in the class. This is to ensure that immature dogs are not rated too highly as early promise is by no means always fulfilled in the adult. When each class is assembled in the ring, exhibits stand in numerical (catalogue) order to facilitate the administration, and the judge goes round checking the mouth of each one and also testicles in the case of dogs. Any individual with missing teeth, or who refuses to have its mouth examined (and a dog who does not have two testicles descended in the scrotum) is disqualified and not graded. By contrast, a dog with extra teeth (usually premolars) is not disqualified!

A careful visual examination of each exhibit follows, with each being moved up and down the ring on a triangular course. The report, with grading, is typed on the official form by the ring secretary who sits at a table in the corner of the ring. All the dogs are then moved round the ring together for varying lengths of time which can be for more than half an hour in the older classes. Since few handlers are Olympic runners, other handlers take over to give a much needed breather. This long perambulation round the ring, much shorter in the case of puppies, is deemed necessary as it separates the dogs with sound conformation from those whose backs 'dip' after exercise, whose movement becomes less true and whose fitness may be in doubt. At the conclusion of the gaiting marathon, the dogs are all placed in order of merit and the critiques handed out. Writing reports on each exhibit takes some time, so the number of dogs which a judge may go over at one time is not much more than 60.

Judges

The ADRK has a training scheme for potential judges of the breed where they start as apprentices. To be considered for this, at least five years' active experience in the breed is necessary, allied to the breeding of typical stock. The would-be judge must be recommended for the apprenticeship by the Club President, have received no convictions in a criminal court (a statement to this effect must be obtained from the police) and must submit a paper on some aspect of the breed set by the Chief Trainer of Judges. Next comes the practical part of the apprenticeship: attending at least six shows under a senior judge of the breed who will discuss the exhibits with the apprentice, stressing important points. The apprentice has to write a report on and grade each exhibit. These are sent to the Chief Trainer of Judges. At the end of the apprenticeship period, the apprentice's reports plus reports from the senior judges are considered by the Judges' Committee which decides whether the apprentice is of a standard suitable to judge. If so, a judge's card is sent by the ADRK and he/she becomes a fully-fledged judge of the breed. This is a great honour as judges have a great influence on the maintenance of breed quality, since the top winners are those most used for breeding. Judging is no hit and miss affair because a judge has an in-depth knowledge of the breed, is familiar with the strengths and weaknesses of lines and is acquainted with a large proportion of dogs and exhibitors entered at shows. Placings are not made merely on the physical appearance and movement of the exhibit on the day of the show, but also on the value of that dog for breeding.

I found being an apprentice judge under the auspices of the ADRK a most interesting, valuable and rewarding experience. I can only reiterate my thanks to Herr Adolf Pienkoss, then President of the ADRK, who agreed to it (I was the first foreigner to apply – and pass) and to the late Friedrich Berger, Chief Breed Warden for many years, my chief mentor, whose great knowledge of the breed was so freely given.

Training and Working Qualifications

The motto of the ADRK is 'Rottweiler breeding is working dog breeding', and tremendous emphasis is placed on temperament and training, great pride being taken in a dog which has a hard, forceful character. Training clubs abound and they are not only the meeting place for Sunday and summer evening training sessions but are also a focus for social activities. Their facilities, equipment and very superior clubhouse, would make them the envy of most societies in this country. The working trials stakes are scheduled under F.C.I. Rules: Schutzhund (abbreviated to SchH) A, SchH I, II and III and Fährtenhunde, FH. With the exception of the first stake, SchHA, which has no tracking, and the FH stake, which consists entirely of tracking, SchH I, II and III include: obedience, agility, gunsure test, tracking and protection. A dog must be at least 14 months old to be entered for the first stake and when it has passed, it proceeds to the next one. The tracking test (FH) may be entered once a dog has obtained the SchH I qualification, the most elementary of the SchH stakes. The maximum points in each stake, including FH, are 100, the pass mark for qualifying in each section is 70% except for protection which is 80%. To qualify, the dog must receive a pass mark in each section and gradings are given according to the total marks awarded: Unsatisfactory, Insufficient, Satisfactory, Good, Very Good, Excellent. Judges for these working tests also receive a comprehensive training before they are approved to officiate at Schützhund and Tracking Trials.

It can be appreciated that the Rottweiler scene in Germany is very different from our own, with a system of control of breeding, registration and training which is unlikely ever to be enforced here. There is only ever one club for a breed, which may have regional branches if that breed is strong enough numerically, as in the case of Rottweilers. The ADRK appoints several officials to oversee the activities of the Club and ensure the breed is proceeding on the right lines. These officials are the President, Vice-President, Chief Breed Warden, Chief Training Warden and Chief Judge. These five people have a continuous watching brief on the breed and may institute changes in the breeding regulations, e.g. dogs must now have a certain hip status to be considered suitable for breeding (apart from conformity to the breed standard). Also, two fairly recent innovations are: no dog or bitch which has incorrect pigmentation of the inner lips and gums (a 'pink' mouth) may receive a grading of Excellent, however beautiful it may be; and a dog or bitch may be entered for the test of suitability for breeding (protection section) as many times as it is necessary for it to pass or the owner wishes. This last stipulation is a surprising and rather disquieting development.

Critics of such an authoritarian system whereby animals must be approved for breeding find fault with it on various levels. The most usual complaints are 'Nobody is going to tell me what to do' or 'It throws the baby out with the bathwater'. Whatever one's opinion, it must be conceded that the quality of the upper echelons of dogs and bitches in Germany is outstanding. Ceaseless efforts are made to ensure that each succeeding generation conforms to the standard in external appearance, in basic character and in soundness. These are three indivisible qualities which make up the essential Rottweiler.

2 History of the Rottweiler in England

The first Dogs

No trace can be found of any Rottweiler being imported and registered with the Kennel Club here before 1936 when the late Mrs Thelma Gray of the famous Rozavel kennels brought in two adult bitches from Germany. First came Diana v. Amalienburg and shortly after Enne v. Pfalzgau, in whelp to Sieger Ido v. Köhlerwald. She had become acquainted with the breed when visiting shows in Germany and had been greatly impressed by its appearance and character. Diana, a very lovely bitch, was sold to a Mrs Simmons before she was released from quarantine and was subsequently well placed at shows. Enne also changed hands before leaving quarantine – her new owner was a Miss Paton. Unfortunately, her litter by Ido contracted distemper before leaving quarantine and, very sadly, all except one died. This bitch, Anna from Rozavel, went to Mrs Gray and, trained by the late Bob Montgomery, proved to be an outstandingly good worker, attracting many admirers and qualifying CDex as well as receiving many top placings in the beauty ring, including Best of Breed at Cruft's 1939.

Mrs Gray then imported a five-month-old dog puppy, Arnolf v.d. Eichener Ruine, and a bitch puppy, Asta v. Norden, a half brother and sister sired by Bruno v.d. Burghalde, with their dams being, respectively, Alma (Nikolaus) and Bella v. Kaltental. Arnolf also proved himself in the show ring. Mrs Gray's last import was a really outstanding German bitch, Int. Ch. Vefa v. Köhlerwald who was mated before she came into the country, but the litter of ten all died in quarantine. Two other Rottweilers, both dogs, were brought over in 1938, Arbo v. Gaisburg by Mrs Simmons and Benno v. Köhlerwald by Miss Homan.

In the three years since their introduction into England the breed had attracted very favourable attention from the public. The early enthusiasts, once referred to by Mrs Gray as 'The Pathfinders', had made every effort to ensure that the foundation stock was of the highest quality, good all-round dogs, adhering closely to the breed

Mrs Thelma Gray
with her prize-
winning Rottweilers
in 1936.

standard in looks, soundness and character, and their success in both
the show ring and in working events is greatly to the credit of those
involved. World War II effectively brought to an end the first chapter
of the Rottweiler in England. Anna from Rozavel and Benno v.
Köhlerwald went to the Armed Forces, and although both survived
the war, Anna living to a ripe old age with her wartime handler, they
were both too old to be used for breeding. At the outbreak of war,
Mrs Gray had to leave her home, which was requisitioned by the
Canadian Army, and she sent her Rottweilers to Eire, with the exception of Anna, on the understanding that they, or their progeny, would
be returned to her after the end of the war. But this was not to be;
they vanished into thin air and all efforts to trace them failed. Mrs
Gray did not import any more Rottweilers and although she retained
her interest in the breed, holding the office of President of the Rottweiler Club for many years, it was only after she emigrated to Australia in 1976 that she owned one again.

The Second Instalment

It was not until 1953 that the Rottweiler was re-introduced into England. A young veterinary surgeon, Captain Frederick Roy-Smith, serving with the Army of Occupation in Germany in the Royal Army Veterinary Corps, had seen the breed under service conditions and had been greatly taken, like Mrs Gray before him, with its looks, temperament and working ability. As a result, when he left the service to return to private practice he brought back with him a dog, Ajax v. Führenkamp and a bitch, Berny v. Weyher. She was neither a top-class specimen nor a good brood bitch and the one live pup she

Captain F. Roy-Smith MRCVS with the first post-war imports: Ajax v. Fuhrenkamp and Berry v. Weyher, both from Germany.

produced was not used for breeding as Captain Roy-Smith did not consider him to be of sufficient merit – a very altruistic decision. He brought in a second bitch, Rintelna (his affix) Lotte v. Osterburg, a very typical, quality bitch. Ajax and Lotte produced two litters, the first in 1958 containing five dogs, four of which, regrettably, went to India and Pakistan while only one remained – Rintelna The Bombardier who was my first Rottweiler. Only one survived from the second litter, a bitch, Rintelna The Chatelaine, who left no progeny in this country before she went to Australia with the Roy-Smith family.

Rudi Eulenspiegel of Mallion. Mrs Joanna Chadwick's foundation dog.

The next person to import Rottweilers was Mrs Joanna Chadwick whose suffix was 'of Mallion'. Frl. Marianne Bruns, a noted German breeder, sent over Rudi Eulenspiegel of Mallion and Quinta Eulenspiegel of Mallion as a breeding pair. They were most prolific and produced some notable progeny, usually very large and greatly divergent in type. Abelard of Mallion was the first Rottweiler to serve in a police force, the Metropolitan of Greater London. Handled by P.C. (later Inspector) Roy Hunter, he made some noteworthy arrests and had a really tough character. Sadly, he died at the age of seven years, on the day after his retirement from official duties. Another Rudi-Quinta son, Brutus, from the 'B' litter also went to the Metropolitan Police and built up a formidable reputation.

Two litter mates from the third Rudi-Quinta litter, born in August 1957, Bruin and Brunnhilde of Mallion were the first Rottweilers to achieve Best in Show awards (at Open Shows). Bruin belonged to Mrs Maud Wait ('Lenlee') who showed and worked him most successfully, bringing the breed to the notice of a wider public. In fact he became the first Rottweiler Working Trials Champion, gaining the qualifications CD, UDex, TDex – a great achievement. Mr and Mrs Garland ('Pilgrimsway') who owned Brunnhilde, also worked her in Obedience. A dog from the last Mallion litter, Erich of Mallion born in 1960, became a champion at the age of 7 years. He was owned by Miss Cook.

Other Mallions acquitted themselves with distinction: Miss Cole's Alberich of Mallion was the first post-war Rottweiler to qualify in working trials; Mrs Gawthrop's Adda of Mallion was always placed well at shows and went with her owner to South Africa.

Quinta had only one litter by a dog other than Rudi, and that by Captain Roy-Smith's Ajax v. Führenkamp. A very nice dog from the litter, Caspar of Mallion, went to Mrs Joan Wheatcroft (Argolis), a staunch supporter of the breed. He was a very handsome dog and did well in the show-ring. Mated to Mrs Wheatcroft's bitch, Anne of Mallion, the two litters included Argolis Ettare, qualified CDex by her owner, then Sgt. Blundy. Her first litter was by Rudi and the best bitch from it, Portlaynum Brigitte, was the foundation bitch of Mr and Mrs Elsden's Chesara kennels.

Another bitch from the Eulenspiegel kennel, Bim Eulenspiegel, was imported in 1958 by Mrs Chadwick in partnership with Mr Newton, but she changed hands shortly after leaving quarantine, going into the ownership of Mrs Wait and Miss Cole. Bim was totally different in type from Rudi and Quinta, being much smaller (even though her sire, Bundessieger Arras v. d. Kappenburgerheide was an extremely large dog) and very lively. Her daughter, by Rudi, Lenlee Neeruam Brigitte, owned by Mrs Wait, qualified CDex and UDex; Brigitte, mated to WT Ch. Bruin of Mallion, produced the second Rottweiler Working Trials Champion, Lenlee Gladiator, CDex, UDex, TDex, PDex, owned and trained by Mrs Osborne (now Buckle).

Little further growth took place in the 1950s. The breed did not 'take off', rather it 'settled in', attracting a certain amount of attention as new breeds usually do, and a few stalwarts who remain owners and/or breeders today. In 1955, one litter (of one puppy) was born while in 1959 there were four litters, producing a total of twenty-one puppies. No-one at that time had the remotest idea of what was in store for the breed and the extraordinary interest which led to the growing registrations of the 1970s and 1980s.

The next decade saw the continued growth of the breed, the granting of challenge certificates by the Kennel Club in 1966 and a number of imports, some of which were to have a far-reaching influence. The first to enter quarantine was the bitch Vera v. Filstalstrand (Castor v. Schussental SchH 1 – Bella v. Remstal) in whelp to the very highly regarded German dog, Droll v.d. Brötzinger-Gasse SchHII. She was owned in partnership by Captain Roy-Smith and myself. Alas, the resultant litter of eight was reduced to three as Vera was so unsettled by quarantine that she killed five which was a tragedy for us. Of the three survivors, Rintelna The Dragoon went to Australia along with Rintelna The Chatelaine when the Roy-Smith family emigrated in 1964; Rintelna The Detective went to the police, and I kept the only bitch, Anouk from Blackforest, a very lively character who proved to be an excellent brood bitch, producing very typical and sound progeny to the three different dogs to which she was mated. Her third litter to Rintelna The Bombardier CDex, UDex had two champions in it, my own Horst CDex, the first champion with a working trials qualification, and Miss Elizabeth Harrap's ('Amerfair') foundation bitch, Hildegard. Another bitch from this combination, Elsa from Blackforest went to Mrs Carol Joseph ('Bhaluk') as her foundation bitch. Elsa's brother, Emil from Blackforest (later CDex), was Mrs Blackmore's ('Gamegards') first Rottweiler and he was the first of her film dogs, acquitting himself with credit in TV, films and advertisements. For a long time Anouk held the record for the longest lived Rottweiler in England; she came within one week of her fourteenth birthday, but a granddaughter of hers, Mr and Mrs Martin's Bhaluk Princess Demeter, was 14 years 7 months old when she died in 1984.

Holland was the source of four of the 1960s imports: Mr Britton's Ajax v.d. Lonneker Bult (Herold v. Kaltenbrunen – Casta), Mrs Elsden's Chesara Luther (Dutch Ch. Baldur v. Habenichts – Astrida) who was to become the first Rottweiler dog champion, Mrs Wait's Lenlee Cabiria v.h. Brabantpark (Ajax v.d. Brantsberg – Ch. Rona v.d. Brantsberg), and Brons, a family pet who accompanied his owners when they decided to settle in England.

Unfortunately, Ajax, a medium-sized, substantial dog, sired only two litters and Cabiria produced but one, to Luther. Luther, a tall dog with a very pleasing head, was widely used at stud and, mated to bitches containing Mallion lines, produced large offspring, and he sired three champions.

A son of the outstanding German dog, International Champion and Bundessieger 1961/2/3 Harras v. Sofienbusch SchHI arrived from the

States in 1964: Blackforest Rodsdens Jett v. Sofienbusch out of American Ch. Afra v. Hasenacker, was a large dog with a powerful driving movement. But the potential promised by his illustrious pedigree was not to be realised; due to some upsetting experiences after leaving quarantine, he did not like showing and he sired but two litters. As his importer, I greatly regretted this for myself and for the breed. The most influential dog of the decade arrived from Sweden in 1965. This was Mrs Elsden's Chesara Akilles (Int. Ch. Fandangos Fairboy – Dackes Ina), who was completely different in type from Luther and the Mallion lines. In size he was small to medium with a short, strong back and a lively extrovert manner. His head was very attractive, having a short, deep, broad muzzle. Only days after leaving quarantine, Akilles went Best in Show at an Open Show and became a champion extremely quickly. His record as a producer was excellent: he sired ten champions and many other prize-winners. Probably his most influential son was Mrs Wallett's Poirot Brigadier who, although he did not gain his title, sired stock of a very pleasing type.

The most influential dog of the 1960s, Mrs Elsden's Ch. Chesara Akilles.

An adult bitch from Germany was brought into the country about the same time as Akilles; she was Blanka v. Östertal (Bodo v.d. Heiden SchH1 – Cara v. Leopoldsthal) a medium-sized bitch of very steady character. Her mating to Ch. Horst from Blackforest CDex produced Mrs Boyd's Ch. Retsacnal Gamegards Gallant Attempt who worked with distinction in Open (All-breed) Obedience competitions.

One of the most notable German dogs of the time was Bundessieger 1966/7 Emir v. Freienhagen SchH3 whose temperament matched his show and working record. Two puppies sired by him, Mr Baldwin's Ero v. Buchaneck (later to become a champion) out of Indra v. Schloss-Westerwinkel and Mrs Blackmore's Gamegards Basula v. Sachenhertz, out of Asta v. Bollerbach, were imported in 1967. Ero was widely used at stud and sired two champions, while Basula took to life as a film star. Both of them excelled in temperament; they were totally 'honest' and the best of companions to their owners. The second import by the Gamegards kennels was a dog who, although he died at the early age of two, had a far-reaching influence on the breed as he proved to be most dominant for sound hips. Gamegards Lars v.d. Hobertsberg (Caro v. Kupferdach SchH3 – Adda v. Dahl SchH3) was a great-grandson of the famous Int. Ch. Harras v. Sofienbusch and his early death was a great misfortune for the breed as he had so much to give. Mrs Blackmore soon sought a replacement for Lars and so it was that Gamegards Bulli v. d. Waldachquelle (Int. Ch. Bulli v. Hungerbuhl SchH2 – Anka v. Reichenbachle) came to England, and he was to prove enormously influential in the development of the breed. He was medium sized, powerfully built, with a broad and attractive head; qualities he passed on to a high proportion

Gamegards Bulli v.d. Waldachquelle, Mrs Blackmore's influential dog who sired six champions.

Mr and Mrs Radley's Ch. Castor of Intisari at 18 months.

of his many offspring, for he was extensively used at stud. At the early age of five he succumbed to a heart attack, but in the comparatively short span of his breeding life he certainly stamped his mark on the breed, siring six champions, including Mr Martin's Ch. Princess Malka of Bhaluk CDex UDex, the first champion Rottweiler bitch to gain working qualification, Mrs Bloom's Ch. Janbicca The Superman, winner of 14 challenge certificates and Mr Gedge's Ch. Prince Gelert of Bhaluk who won 12 certificates. Superman sired four champions, including two from one litter and also the Sussex police dog, Blitz of Pixtonhill.

Altogether, the 1960s saw about sixteen imports, some of which were companion animals returning to England with their owners while others were imported with a view to making a specific contribution to the breed. One such was the Danish dog, Castor of Intisari, later champion (Int. Ch. Farro v.h. Brabantpark SchH2 - Danish Ch. Ursula PH AK) brought in by Mr and Mrs Radley whose paternal great-grandsire was Int. Ch. Harras v. Sofienbusch SchH1. He was another medium-sized, substantial dog with a very strong back. He excelled in temperament and was most prepotent for sound hips, siring four champions. His lines are mainly carried on through Ch. Linguards Norge, a prolific sire.

In the 1970s, two other dogs, both from Germany, were widely used at stud: Mr Gordon McNeill's Ausscot Hasso v. Märchenwald, later champion (Int. Ch. Elko v. Kastanienbaum SchH1 - Cora v.

Reichenbachle), who sired four champions, including one from a mating to his daughter. The other dog was Mrs Hughes' Lord v.d. Grurmannsheide of Herburger (Carlo v.d. Simonskaul SchH1 – Asta v.d. Bolt) who was mated with two bitches, carrying Chesara and Gamegards lines, to form the foundation of the Herburger kennel. Lord possessed a good genotype for hip conformation. Later, this kennel imported a puppy from the States, Herburger Arno v. Ross (American Ch. Kirk v. Cratty – Olga v. Ruhrstrom), a very typical medium sized, compact dog with a most attractive head and very steady temperament. He has been used mainly on Herburger bitches.

Mrs Hughes' Herburger Arno v. Ross imported from the USA.

Another import from Germany, Catja v.d. Flugschneise (Chris v.d. Wildberger Schloss SchH2 – Britta v. Frielicker Landhaus SchH1), went on to Australia after the statutory quarantine and residence period, but, before doing so, produced a litter to Ch. Castor of Intisari, five of which remained in this country. Three were used for breeding and the progeny had a good record for hip and forehand soundness.

A litter brother and sister imported by Mrs Elsden from the famous Triomfator kennels in Holland, Torro and Tara Triomfator, have proved enormously influential through their descendants. Torro's sons, Ch. Chesara Dark Roisterer and Ch. Upend Gallant Gairbert sired numerous litters and the former's son, Ch. Pendley Goldfinch, was also used extensively. But it is through their descendant, Ch. Chesara Dark Charles (Tara is the granddam on the sire's side and Torro great-grandsire on the dam's side) that the greatest influence so far has come. Apart from siring some really outstanding stock, the wide introduction of the Triomfator lines through Charles has proved particularly beneficial for hips, as seen by the results from the official British Veterinary Association/Kennel Club Hip Dysplasia Scheme. One of Charles's sons, Ch. Caprido Minstrel of Potterspride, owned by Mrs Slade, has also proved to be a sire of top-class stock.

A dog and bitch imported from Belgium, Breesegata's Dago and Breesegata's Finny, produced no progeny, and a bitch from Sweden, Sangetts Villa Zayonara had only two litters before dying of a penicillin allergy at an early age. This was a great pity as the pedigrees of all three carried some illustrious lines.

Not all imports are able to make a really positive contribution to the breed, which is unfortunate, as our period of quarantine, vital though it is, makes importing a costly business and limits the number of dogs which come into the country.

Two imports came in from Germany on their way to Australia in the early 1980s: Colonel Pettengell's Felix v. Magdeberg (Brando v. Hause Neubrand SchH3 – Biene v. Hohenhameln SchH3) and Echo v. Magdeberg. Felix sired one litter to Ch. Nobane Bianka before leaving the country, and another dog, also en route to Australia, the American-bred Powderhorn Fetz of Wencrest (Ch. Oscar v.h. Brabantpark – Illona v. Hause Schottroy) sired two litters, one to a bitch of Herburger lines.

Of the two dogs which came in from Sweden, one, Ranco from Svedala, was not used for breeding, and the other, Bergsgardens Samson of Gregarth (Larry v. Stüffelkopf – Ambra) was used extensively, but it is too early to assess his long-term contribution to the breed. One of the latest imports is the German bitch Fella v. Siegerlenpflad, very well constructed and typical who returned to this country with an army family, Mr and Mrs Hosband.

The pioneer breeders are no longer active; Captain Roy-Smith died in Australia in 1981, and Mrs Joanna Chadwick did not re-enter the show or breeding scene after her children grew up. Apart from Mr Kelly, in N. Ireland, the only two of the second wave of early breeders still involved are Mrs Elsden ('Chesara') who came into the breed in 1962 and me ('Blackforest'). I owned my first Rottweiler in 1958. The Chesara kennels is certainly the most successful in this country, having produced many champions at home and overseas and numerous other winners. Mrs Elsden was Top Breeder (Dog World Table) in 1983, and Ch. Chesara Dark Charles the Top Stud Dog (All Breeds) for the same year. The Blackforests are a very much smaller opera-

Ch. Chesara Dark Destiny. The first English Rottweiler Ch., bred and owned by Mrs Elsden whose Chesara Kennels is the most successful Rottweiler kennels in the UK.

tion, with a dual-purpose emphasis, having at this time the greatest in-depth working pedigree. From here came the first Champion to qualify in Working Trials, Ch. Horst from B. CDex (Rintelna The Bombardier – Anouk from Blackforest).

During the mid-1970s, public attention increasingly focused on the breed which led to more and more litters being bred until there was nothing less than a population explosion, with a huge influx of 'breeders' anxious not to miss out on any financial pickings to be had from a breed which takes the public's fancy. To the concerned, caring and enlightened breeder, undue popularity is a curse to a breed. It brings many problems such as the advent of those with no primary interest apart from moneymaking, the use of sub-standard stock for breeding, the incidence of defects which are manifested as a result of imprudent or random matings, and too many puppies chasing too few suitable homes. This last point can cause problems through mismatching the dog and owner. As a result animals transgress and the more serious incidents are reported in the media which erodes the reputation of the breed.

Indeed, the early post-war days of the Rottweiler in England are very far removed from the present boom in the breed. Then, with the small numbers, it was easy to keep track of developments; bloodlines had not become so mixed and diluted to make it difficult to know (or guess even) what characteristics lines carried and the likely breeding potential. People owned or bred Rottweilers because they really liked the breed and financial gain was not uppermost in their minds.

However, one thing is certain, public favour can be fickle and meteoric rises in popularity, as in the case of the Rottweiler, can be followed by equally dramatic falls to a sensible and manageable level of interest.

3 Development of the Standard

The origins of the Rottweiler are considered to lie in the herding dogs known in Roman times. These dogs seem to have accompanied the legions to protect and drive cattle over the Alps, and were found along the military routes of the period and later along the trade routes. There were three types: (1) Molossian (modern equivalent, Komondor and Pyrenean); (2) bristly coated herd dogs (Swiss Sennenhunde, Rottweiler); (3) bristly coated wolflike-shepherd dogs (German, French and Belgian Shepherds).

Before the advent of shows, a dog's value was decided solely upon the efficiency with which he performed a specific function or functions, and the aim of breeding was to improve physical and mental characteristics in order to improve the dog's capability for work. The demands placed upon dogs were much greater than they are today, and any animal not meeting these requirements was ruthlessly discarded.

Considerable changes have taken place in the external form of the descendants of these early herding dogs and, as far as Rottweilers were concerned, there were two types. There was a larger, stronger animal primarily used as companions and guards by cattle drovers as not only were they less agile but also they tended to 'nip' too high up on the legs of any wayward beast, and a smaller, quicker type of dog employed for droving purposes.

Over the centuries, crossings with other breeds took place and even within the last 100/150 years it is believed that crossings between the Rottweiler and varieties of Swiss Sennenhunde, Great Danes and Mastiffs occurred, but positive proof is unlikely to be found since such matings were not documented. Reference to the standard of the Bernese Mountain Dog reveals a striking similarity to that of the Rottweiler.

Controversies between the early German Rottweiler breed clubs, mentioned in Chapter 1, arose because of differing views on how the Rottweiler should be constructed, for once a standard had been published and a club formed planned breeding was started, to produce a dog of strength and nobility, without coarseness, capable of retaining its working function. In 1933 it seemed that the political regime in power in Germany might change the role of the Rottweiler into that of a super 'messenger' dog, but due to the opposition from breeders, these plans came to nought.

Hans Korn, writing in the special booklet issued on the occasion of the 50th Anniversary of the ADRK in 1957, states that Rottweilers were entered at dog shows in Germany in the 1880s, albeit in small numbers. The following description of the breed which appeared in Count van Bylandt's Book, *Breeds of Dogs*, published in Holland in 1894, shows that the breed was very different in those days.

'Rottweiler – German Cattle Dog

GENERAL APPEARANCE: A dog of medium size, strongly built, rather coarse.

HEAD: Of medium length; skull broad and dome-shaped; stop well defined; muzzle rather short; lips not too pendulous; nose black; nostrils well opened; teeth strong and meeting evenly.

EYES: Large and round; dark brown in colour; expression grave and intelligent.

EARS: Of medium size, close to the head; triangular in shape.

NECK: Short, strong and muscular, well arched; dew-laps not too much developed.

BODY: Strongly built; shoulders sloping; chest very broad and deep; back straight; ribs well rounded; loins short and muscled; belly slightly drawn up; hindquarters short.

LEGS: Straight and muscular, well set under the body; elbows close to the body; stifles high and straight.

FEET: Not too short, but well closed; dewclaws objectionable.

TAIL: A bobtail is preferable, otherwise the tail is of medium length and very strong, carried low or slightly upwards.

COAT: Short, dense and hard, longer on the legs and at the tail, shorter and smooth on the ears.

COLOUR: Black with yellow markings; yellow with black markings and blue merle with black patches and yellow markings; white patches on skull, chest and legs permissible.

HEIGHT AT SHOULDER: About 23½ inches.

WEIGHT: About 65 lbs.

FAULTS: Narrow skull; long muzzle; flews; small and folded ears; light eyes; long, lean and light body; long coat and lean tail.'

The first standard, formulated by Albert Kull of the International Club for Leonbergers and Rottweiler Dogs, was not published until 1901. It calls for a medium-to-large, square-built dog, with bitches always smaller and longer in the back. Eyes were to be dark brown, medium sized, full with fiery, intelligent expression. Steep shoulders

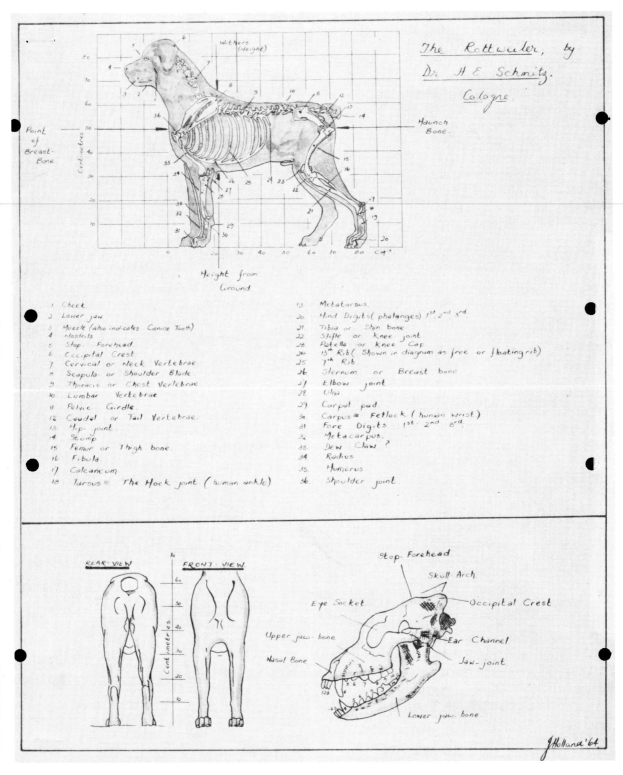

The Rottweiler, by Dr. H E Schmitz. Cologne.

1. Cheek.
2. Lower jaw.
3. Muzzle (also indicates Canine Tooth)
4. Nostrils.
5. Stop. Forehead.
6. Occipital Crest.
7. Cervical or Neck Vertebrae.
8. Scapula or Shoulder Blade.
9. Thoracic or Chest Vertebrae.
10. Lumbar Vertebrae.
11. Pelvic Girdle.
12. Caudal or Tail Vertebrae.
13. Hip-joint.
14. Stump.
15. Femur or Thigh bone.
16. Fibula.
17. Calcaneum.
18. Tarsus = The Hock joint. (human ankle)
19. Metatarsus.
20. Hind Digits (phalanges) 1st, 2nd, 3rd.
21. Tibia or Shin bone.
22. Stifle or Knee joint.
23. Patella or Knee Cap.
24. 13th Rib (Shown in diagram as free or floating rib)
25. 7th Rib.
26. Sternum or Breast bone.
27. Elbow joint.
28. Ulna.
29. Carpal pad.
30. Carpus = Fetlock (human wrist)
31. Fore Digits 1st, 2nd, 3rd.
32. Metacarpus.
33. Dew Claw. ?
34. Radius.
35. Humerus.
36. Shoulder joint.

J Holland '64

were called for, with a short upper arm, and hindquarters were to be steep with high hocks. Greatly to be desired was the natural 'stumpy' tail, otherwise the tail was to be docked to medium length, carried high and at a steep angle.

The coat was unusually thick with profuse undercoat and several colours were permitted: black with rust or yellow markings (the most common), black stripes on an ash grey background with yellow markings, plain red with a black nose, dark wolf grey with black head and saddle but always with yellow markings. White markings on chest and legs permissible if not too extensive.

A more comprehensive standard with a system of points allocation to the various physical features was published by the International Rottweiler Club in 1913. The demand was still for a square dog, as compact as possible. Changes were made in that eyelids were to fit closely; the pastern joint to be powerful and supple rather than too steep and as straight as possible; and docked tail held in a straight line with the back. Variations in colour were still permitted: black with rust or orange markings, also brown with yellow markings, blue or plain red with black mask and black line down the back. The coat was described as thick, hard and bristly, as short as possible with a minimum of light undercoat.

In 1914 the DRK published its own standard, broadly similar to that of the IRC but less detailed or clear. Size was obviously a matter of contention for in the IRC standard dogs were to be 60–65 cms and bitches 55–65, whereas the DRK stipulated dogs were to be from 58–66 cms and bitches 55–63.

The two clubs amalgamated in 1921 to form the Allgemeiner Deutscher Rottweiler Klub and another standard for the breed was compiled. This was a combination of both standards, with descriptions of features taken from each. An important development was that there was only one colour permitted, black with tan markings, and although small white markings on chest and belly were allowed, they were not desirable. Height range was modified, with dogs being 60–68 cms and bitches 55–65 cms. Rewritten again after World War II, the new standard closely resembled the one which preceded it, but in the introduction it is stated that the dog should not be too short in build, while under the heading of General Appearance, a compact, strong and well-proportioned frame is required. For the first time the section on faults was divided into two sections, beauty faults, e.g. light or round eyes, loose skin on throat, and working faults, e.g. flat feet, long in back. A new German (FCI) standard was published in 1970, far more comprehensive than any of the others and this is shown at Appendix 3. The height range for dogs remained 60–65 cms while that for bitches was changed to 55–63 cms and the length from breastbone to point of rump should not exceed the height at the withers by more than 15%. A very long section on character appears for the first time. One feature common to all the previous standards was reference to the sterling qualities of the Rottweiler's character – courage, incorruptibility as a watchdog, loyalty, high intelligence, eagerness to work, and good nature. Emphasis is placed on the traits which make the breed a devoted companion and top-class working dog, for the ADRK's motto is 'Rottweiler breeding is working dog breeding'.

The 1970 standard goes much further, listing the desirable instincts and character attributes, with degree of intensity, which fit the Rottweiler so well for those roles. Such a development is in line with current thinking in the country of origin where the importance of maintaining the ability to work is implemented by having a minimum qualification necessary for the higher suitability for breeding grading, Körung (or Selection), and for entry in the Gebrauchshundklasse (Working Dog Class) at shows.

All breeds recognised by official Kennel Clubs have a breed standard which describes in detail its physical and mental characteristics, an image of perfection for which a breeder should aim, and against which a judge evaluates exhibits presented at shows. Without a breed standard there would be no correct type and, of course, shows provide the opportunity for breeders to compare their stock with that of others.

Nowadays, apart from the FCI standard, there are several others (American, English, Canadian) which differ in form of presentation, and in length, that of the FCI used in Germany, the country of origin, being the most comprehensive and lengthy, and it is the evolution of this with which we are mainly concerned. The original English standard was taken from the German one current at the time, but when the breed was allocated challenge certificates, it was revised to conform with Kennel Club format. As has already been mentioned, the present English standard is much shorter than the German one; a brief discussion follows on some features.

General Appearance
While the Rottweiler is above average in size, as a working dog he should have a compact and sturdy body, showing no trace of clumsiness or coarseness of build. He should give an impression of vigour, power and strength. A marked difference in build exists between males and females, with the former being larger and more heavily built with stronger bone.

Character/Temperament
Although the standard is quite specific regarding mental attributes,

the fact that the Rottweiler is a guard breed must never be overlooked. One cannot have it all ways and differences in reactions from, say, hound or gundog breeds are to be expected: Rottweilers do not take kindly to overhandling or undue familiarity by strangers so it is essential to train a dog to expect to be handled by a veterinary surgeon or judge, however much the dog may resent it, and to guard it from demonstrative excesses by those not known to it.

The Head

The head of the Rottweiler should show much nobility, even grandeur. It is of medium length and the proportions are - tip of nose to inner corner of eye to occiput - 2:3. The stop is well defined unlike that of the very early dogs which had hound-like heads, and when viewed from the side, the skull shows a moderate arch. The small ears should be set high, but not like those of a terrier, so making the skull appear broader. The muzzle should be well filled beneath the eye, deep and with a level bridge of nose. Lips should be black and tight; droopiness at the corners is an unattractive feature. An almond-shaped eye is called for, dark brown in colour, and lids should be close fitting. The expression is all important and should be indicative of confidence and dignity.

In Germany, rose-coloured inner lips and gums are regarded as serious faults. While those of some dogs may start out dark, age may bring increasing loss of colour.

The head should be 'dry' i.e. skin fits tightly, although when the dog is alert the skull may show lengthwise wrinkles. The neck is very strong and muscular, with a slight arch, free from throatiness. In dogs of very compact build, the neck may be rather short ('stuffy') since the length of bones in the body bear relation to each other. Too long a neck is equally undesirable.

Teeth

The teeth should be large, strong and correctly aligned (scissors bite), and all should be present (42). Faulty occlusion of the teeth in extreme cases causes difficulty in picking up and eating food and excessive wearing of the teeth. A pincer (edge-to-edge) bite is undesirable as it also causes wearing.

Body

A substantial, compact body is required with scarcely perceptible tuck-up, and a level, well-muscled back which remains stable in movement (does not dip or roach). But to have a totally rigid back is not anatomically feasible and there must be a degree of flexibility. The broad, deep chest ideally should be 50% of the height at the withers.

Legs which are too short frequently go with a heavy, barrel-like body, giving a coarse untypical appearance. Equally untypical are legs which are too long, often accompanying a body that is too narrow. A symmetrical body is wanted: forequarters and hindquarters in balance so that the horizontal view is of equal breadth of shoulder, rib cage and pelvis. Likewise the fore and hind angulation should be equivalent, otherwise the gait is affected; too much bend of stifle allied to a short back results in crabbing and too little a short stride. Research has shown that the 45° angle described as the ideal for the shoulder blades is unrealistic and that is not found.

In order to minimise the concussion sustained when the forelegs strike the ground, a slightly sloping pastern is required since an upright one increases the jarring effect. Weak pasterns are not infrequently seen in Rottweilers and this serious working fault is reflected in movement.

Feet
Feet are as important to a dog as to an army! The open, flat feet with thin pads are a bad fault. Short, well-arched toes with thick hard pads, the so-called cat foot, with short, dark nails, are required.

Coat and Markings
The Rottweiler's coat consists of a harsh, medium length topcoat, flat and straight, always black with tan markings and an undercoat. Faults of texture, too soft or too bristly, are found as well as too long and too wavy a coat. Pale, straw-coloured markings are unattractive as are too extensive markings which are occasionally seen, sometimes even extending up the front legs, on the hindlegs and on the bridge of the nose. Conversely, the tan areas may lack definition, having black hairs interspersed with the tan or being too small in extent. The undercoat, which may be grey, fawn or black, sometimes shows through when the dog is casting its coat, but otherwise it should not be visible. Lack of undercoat is a fault; this is usually associated with too short a coat. In very hot countries, the dog adapts to conditions by not growing an undercoat.

White markings, which are undesirable, most frequently appear on the chest, in the centre of the 'handlebars'. A fair indication of whether they are likely to disappear may be gained by checking to see if the skin beneath the white hair is lacking in pigment.

Size
An important factor to remember about size is that the FCI standard and the American standard permit a greater variation in height than the English one:

FCI standard dogs $23\frac{3}{4}$–27 inches bitches $21\frac{3}{4}$–$25\frac{3}{4}$ inches
American ,,   ,,   24–27   ,,   ,,   22–25   ,,
English   ,,   ,,   25–27   ,,   ,,   23–25   ,,

I regard this as unfortunate. Virtue should not be measured by the inch or pound, and animals at either end of the size continuum are equally typical provided that the other specifications of the standard are met. Whatever the size, a dog must look masculine and a bitch feminine.

When evaluating a Rottweiler what should be at the forefront of the mind is that it is a working breed and while the English standard does not differentiate between construction or working faults and cosmetic ones, those which adversely affect its ability to work should be regarded more seriously than faults which do not.

4   Is a Rottweiler for you?

Choice of a breed should be dictated by a number of factors, including financial provision for a dog's maintenance, feeding, licensing, insurance and veterinary fees, interior and exterior space available at home, time that can be spent on exercising, socialising and training the puppy or adult, the ability of the individual to understand and cope with the varying demands of different types of dogs (hounds, toys, terriers, giant and guard-breeds) and last but not least, personal preference, which draws one to a particular breed, often for emotional reasons.

It is this last reason which takes precedence when the final choice is made, and whilst of course there should be a strong attraction towards a breed, the success or otherwise of the relationship between dog and owner depends primarily on the other points mentioned.

Financial considerations are very important with large or giant breeds since they require good feeding in order to achieve healthy adulthood, especially during the period of rapid growth. In the case of Rottweilers this is from about 1–8 months. Good feeding means a balanced diet, be it a complete food or fresh meat (when vitamin and mineral supplements are required as well as milk, egg yolk and biscuit) given in sufficient quantities to keep the growing animal well covered but *not* fat.

Veterinary fees can be expensive with a large breed if an operation is required or the dog has a serious illness, and it is best to take out insurance, but there will still be the cost of annual booster inoculations which are essential.

Rottweilers are certainly not recommended for flat life or a very small home without a garden; it can be trying for dog and owner and bringing up a puppy is extraordinarily demanding. Pups do chew and make messes. Without a garden the energy of a pup has to be worked off somehow and this can be on the furniture, carpets etc!

The Rottweiler is highly intelligent, extremely protective of his home and family, affectionate and very steady. His strength, power and guarding abilities mean that he must be socialised (given as much experience of the outside world and all its complexities) as early as possible during puppyhood, as well as trained in manners and the responses expected of any dog in our urbanised society.

Lending a hand with the shopping, Mr Thompson's Nytecharm Satan.

The untrained Rottweiler can be a menace, sometimes a dangerous menace, and it is vital that the training given is firm but kind. Rottweilers are in no way a submissive breed and, to get the best out of them, training should be made fun with generous praise and reward. Hard physical punishment is counterproductive and only brings out the stubborn side of the dog's character. A mental tug-of-war between dog and human will be the result instead of the rapport which is so rewarding.

While both dogs and bitches exhibit the same temperamental traits, the Rottweiler dog is generally much more of a handful, requiring greater understanding and care in training. Inclined to be 'bossy', he needs to know who is 'pack leader' and if this position is established during puppyhood, the relationship between dog and owner should develop smoothly. Sometimes the young dog can go through an adolescent phase from about the age of nine months when he seeks to assert himself over humans and dogs alike, deciding whom he likes and will be friendly towards. This is the time for the owner to firmly direct the dog's behaviour into acceptance and tolerance of other dogs and humans. This is not accomplished overnight; much patience may be necessary on the part of the owner and occasionally the dog may need a sharp tap!

Many male dogs which need to be re-homed find themselves in this position because of behavioural problems which have arisen at the adolescent stage when, due to lack of experience or understanding of the owner, the dog may have shown aggression or even bitten someone. In such a case the owner may lose confidence and may even be frightened of the dog, so it is passed on or put down.

Mrs Jenkins' Lauraston Yankie v. Ilona waiting her turn at a training class.

However, while a male dog may be a little too much for some to handle, the bitch, of smaller size and more malleable in character, may present a most acceptable alternative. There is no doubt that the male is more striking in appearance. He is taller and more substantial with a larger, broader head and an air of quiet arrogance. He appeals most strongly to men because of the 'macho' image he conveys.

The bitch is equally good as a guard but is more affectionate, with much less desire to take on the role of pack leader in the human household, though she may sometimes be intolerant of other bitches.

It should never be forgotten that responsibility for the everyday care and upbringing of a puppy usually falls on the woman of the household and a dog may demand just too much time and attention. Always in the case of an owner new to the breed, it is advisable for the first Rottweiler to be a bitch. Then, if the family becomes 'hooked' on the breed, as often happens, they can take on a male dog, having gained experience with the bitch. Those who have never owned a dog before should definitely start with a bitch. Choice is sometimes made on the basis of a bitch's seasons (usually twice a year) but this problem may be overcome by spaying, always after, *never* before, the first season, or by control through injection.

But whether you have a dog or a bitch Rottweiler, your responsibilities as an owner of a member of the guarding breeds remain the same: fair but firm basic training to make it a respectable member of canine society, and efficent care and maintenance to keep it healthy and not a health hazard in or outdoors. So while a Rottweiler is most certainly a dog for all seasons, it is certainly not a dog for all humans.

Basically the temperament of the breed is extremely sound, and it is a great sadness to see animals which have been spoilt through lack of understanding and care by their owners. In the right hands, the pleasure a handsome, highly intelligent, powerful and active dog gives is immeasurable, but if you do not think you have the time, space, money or personality to cope with a large dog of strong character, then do not buy one for unhappiness and dissatisfaction surely lie ahead for both you and the dog. Some Rottweilers, usually the males, can be extremely aggressive towards other dogs and this is a most unpleasant trait. Early socialisation with other pups and non-aggressive dogs is the answer, allied to careful correction of any show of aggression, and obedience training (i.e. manners training). Prevention of the habit is far, far easier than curing it.

If there is a dog or bitch or another breed in the household, it is usually better to have a second one of the opposite sex, since dogs are more tolerant of bitches than of other dogs and the same applies to bitches. It should not be forgotten that whereas one dog is an individual, two form a pack and can gang up on another dog of either sex, so socialisation with other dogs and bitches should be a training priority.

A very frequent question asked is whether Rottweilers are good with children and the answer to that lies in a counter-question – are the children good with dogs? Certainly the track record of the breed with children seems very good, but it must depend on the attitude of the parents: it is most unfair and unkind to a dog of any breed to permit young children to have unrestricted access to it and not to be shown the correct way of treating dogs. Poking eyes, pulling ears, kicking (and even biting), teasing, especially with food, are *out*. Because of his size, the Rottweiler can unwittingly hurt toddlers by knocking them down in play and the decision on whether or not to introduce a Rottweiler into the family should be influenced by the age of the children, time the mother can spare and space available so the dog can have his own quiet 'den', away from prying fingers.

Mrs M. St Maur Sheil's Badger who is wonderful with children.

Since most dogs at one time or another will interact with children, in or out of their own household, the following points are emphasised as general guidelines with any breed of dog.

1. A child should never tease a dog.
2. A child should respect its den or bed.
3. A child should not disturb the dog when it is asleep or eating.
4. A child should never grab at a strange dog without the permission of the owner and most particularly if it is tied up, for instance outside a shop.
5. Dogs need to be accustomed to young children and the sudden movements and shrill noises they make.
6. Dogs may not like children running past them, including those on roller skates.
7. When a dog is not under supervision, it may bar the path of a child (or adult), growl or bare its teeth. Do not turn and run away but stand still, remain calm and allow the dog to sniff at you.
8. Remember hygiene: accustom the child from the outset always to wash its hands, not to allow itself to be licked, and not to put the dog's ear or paws into its mouth.
9. Many children like to take a dog for a walk. Only dogs which are lead trained and well accustomed to traffic, other people and other

The waiting game. Jack and Liz Brendon's Breckley Soldier Boy CDex UDex and Breckley Brittania.

dogs, and are not excitable should be allowed out with youngsters. Rottweilers should never go out with young children unaccompanied as they are too strong for them.

10. If a puppy is to be brought into a household as a pet, it should be ensured that it has not suffered any prior unfortunate experiences to make it dislike children.

One of the behavioural traits of some Rottweilers, usually males, is their habit of 'talking'. To the uninitiated this is a growl, but there are different notes ranging from the talkative rumble, accompanied by wagging stump and smiling eyes, to the one-note menacing sound which accompanies a 'black' look. This vocal habit is not always understood or liked, and it is up to the owner to check it if it gets out of hand.

Space, time and financial considerations apart, there remains the vital aspect of temperament and all that implies to be considered before making the decision to have a Rottweiler. Mrs Muriel Freeman, the eminent American authority on the breed, wrote 'The Rottweiler is not a toy', and it cannot be emphasised sufficiently that it is a guard breed, with generations of service behind it, having the strong character required for such a role. The adage that there are horses for courses is equally true of dogs: because of its size, power, activity level and strong guarding instincts, the Rottweiler is most certainly not the dog for everyone, particularly those who have not owned a guard breed before, or the indulgent, weak-willed or nervous person who cannot or is not prepared to exert authority to ensure a standard of behaviour in the dog which will make it a pleasure to own and take about. So ask yourself a final question: are you the right sort of person to own a Rottweiler?

5 Choice of Puppy

The points and guidelines which follow really apply to any breed, but in the case of the Rottweiler they are of paramount importance, since many buyers are new to the breed, have no previous experience of guard breeds and, not infrequently, have never owned a dog.

Before any question arises of choice of puppy, the most important consideration is choice of breeder. With rare breeds there may only be very few active breeders, but with Rottweilers one is spoilt for choice. In the early days when the opposite was true, those interested often had to travel long distances for their puppy, as well as often having to wait for many months. Now, with more dogs available a potential buyer should neither have to travel too far nor wait a long time. But one should be flexible in these respects in order to obtain exactly the right puppy. Do not buy a puppy in haste.

In their quest for a puppy people often do not ask enough questions or the right questions of the breeder and often their hearts rule their heads or purses. The conscientious and caring breeder will be happy to show the resident dogs and bitches and discuss their background and characters fully. It goes without saying that you should be able to touch all of them, except of course puppies in the nest, for reasons of possible infection. The breeder's general attitude should be helpful, forthright and concerned that the puppies should go to suitable homes. And with this in mind, you should expect to be asked about yourself, your experience in dogs and what sort of facilities you are able to offer the puppy. Just as you assess the breeder and stock so, too, will you be assessed. If no questions are asked of you about your home and background, then, frankly my advice would be to go elsewhere because that particular breeder does not have the welfare of the puppies in mind and is unlikely to provide a satisfactory after-sales service to the new puppy owners, essential in the case of first-time owners.

Apart from visiting the breeder, potential owners should find out:
1. Whether sire and dam are X-rayed for hip dysplasia and the plates submitted for scoring through the official British Veterinary Association/Kennel Club Scheme. Do not accept the statement 'My vet says they (the hips) are good enough for breeding'. Now that the scoring

scheme is in operation, without the stigma of the 'pass' or 'fail' result, there can be no excuse for not X-raying and if the parents have not been done, then I would have no interest in the litter.

2. Whether sire and dam are registered at the Kennel Club. It is essential to check this fact as it may prove difficult or even impossible to register the puppies if the parents are unregistered, as some owners have found to their cost.

3. The age of sire and dam. Since it is a sad fact of life that animals of all sorts are ready targets for human exploitation, I would not accept a puppy out of a young bitch which was mated at an early age (say under twenty months); ideally the bitch should not be under two years old. At this age, the bitch is usually fully developed physically and mentally. Nor would I accept puppies from a bitch eight years or over; her breeding days should be past by then; she has done her bit for the breed (and the breeder!).

4. Whether the dam has had a litter before. If so, how long ago? Some breeders make a practice of mating a bitch on two or more successive seasons (and in the worst cases every season, to the detriment of bitch and pups). I hold strong views on this subject, and whilst it may be marginally acceptable to breed on a bitch's next season after having only one or at most two pups in a litter, it most certainly is not done with the good of the bitch in mind if she is put into whelp at the first opportunity after having produced a litter of good size. The motive is greed!

5. Show/working record of parents. Have they been shown or worked? It is certainly not a prerequisite for a healthy litter that the parents have been entered at shows or working events. However, in a breed which is numerically strong, dogs and bitches which deviate markedly from the breed standard and have serious conformation faults should not be pressed into service for breeding. Do not accept the excuse 'All bitches should have at least one litter, it is good for them', or 'My vet says a litter will calm her down' or 'make her more confident' etc., etc. Such statements are usually a way of rationalising money-making activities from sub-standard stock.

6. Problems. By no means every breeder is prepared to be frank about such matters and novice breeders may well not have an in-depth knowledge of the background of their stock. But potential purchasers should ask about soundness (apart from hips), any forehand lameness, cruciate ligament rupture and eye problems, in the pedigree.

7. Finally, ensure that you will be given a diet sheet and that the breeder will be happy to answer any questions or deal with any problems that may arise. In other words, the transaction does not end with the payment and the breeder ought to retain an interest in the puppies throughout their lives.

The Puppy

There is an acceptable variation in temperament between bloodlines and between individuals in a litter, thus catering for the requirements and abilities of the would-be owner. A system whereby important temperamental traits may be identified in puppies as young as 49 days has been developed in the United States. In this way, a very dominant and active puppy can be matched with a person who has the personality and experience to ensure he will be the pack-leader, while the more submissive and gentler puppy will be suited to an owner who cannot cope with a demanding, dominant dog. This reduces the likelihood of there being a mismatch between dog and owner which causes dogs to be re-homed or even, in extreme cases, to be destroyed.

Unfortunately, this Puppy Aptitude Test (PAT) is little known in England and, although it has received some publicity, it has attracted little interest. The potential for a large and powerful dog of strong character like the Rottweiler to go wrong and develop undesirable behaviour in the hands of the inexperienced or ignorant, is indeed great, and were breeders to utilise this test in conjunction with a rigorous selection policy applied to would-be owners, then there would be fewer instances of Rottweilers being out of control.

Most puppies go to pet homes and the selection of a puppy when it is left to the buyer alone is often made purely on the appeal exerted by a specific physical characteristic such as 'the largest in the litter', 'lovely bright markings', 'he came to me first', 'she just chose me' and so on. Little or no attempt is made to fit the likely temperament of the puppy to the ability and circumstances of the buyer. This is where the PAT would prove invaluable.

If the litter is raised mostly indoors, with a high degree of family involvement enabling the puppies and their behaviour to be observed for appreciable lengths of time, then the dominant, withdrawn or highly active members of the litter may be identified. It is surprising that more breeders do not utilise the system of easy identification using different coloured thin leather collars round the puppies' necks. Having two-tone colour, it is not always easy to see which puppy is which when they are in the nest, nor does cutting off bits of hair on different parts of the body help very much. However, in a kennel environment there is less time for puppy watching so the breeder has much less to go on if the puppies are to be placed on the basis of likely character.

The Puppy Aptitude Test of which I have experience is one developed by the Americans Wendy and Jack Volhard to identify the dog's basic temperament traits and indicate the one with the most obedience potential which is their main interest. Optimum time for carrying out this test is on the 49th day. A puppy's neurological connections are not complete before the seventh week and from the eighth to tenth week the puppy is in the fear imprint stage (see Chapter 8) when it is vital that it is not frightened. A sympathetic stranger tests the puppies in a part of the breeder's establishment with which they are unfamiliar. Tests alternate between a slightly stressful one and one which is neutral or more pleasurable. The puppy is given a rating on each test, with an average overall rating allocated at the end.

The nine tests are:

Social attraction – indicates social attraction, confidence or dependence. The puppy's attitude to the tester.

Following – a non-follower shows independence, a follower tractability. Whether/how the puppy follows the tester.

Restraint – degree of submission revealed. If held, puppy's reaction.

Social dominance – extent to which puppy accepts social dominance.

Elevation – shows how puppy will react when under stress and has no control of the situation. Puppy held a few inches above floor, supported under chest.

Retrieving – indicates interest in retrieving objects and willingness to work with a human.

Touch Sensitivity
Sound Sensitivity } degree of sensitivity in these modalities.
Sight Sensitivity

Up to the present time no scientific validation of these tests with long term follow-up studies has been carried out which is a pity, and their potential as a tool for placing the right puppy in the right home has hardly been touched upon. Testing allied to observation reveals which pups are dominant/submissive to humans or dogs; which are independent/shy/aggressive; which are quiet/lively; which are alert/dull. Thus the breeder can glean information to enable each puppy to be matched with the most suitable owner, hopefully to ensure a happy, lifelong relationship.

Potential Show Specimens

As far as selecting a potential show dog is concerned, it is advisable first to visit several shows to see what dogs are winning and what types appeal to you. Contacts with show kennels may be made and arrangements to visit. It is important for the potential show owner to find a breeder who has a record of achievement in the show ring and who is prepared to assist in choosing a suitable puppy. Of course, no-one can guarantee that a puppy of 7–8 weeks with everything going for it will develop into a star, but there is much more chance of it doing so if it comes from a background of typical dogs. Advertisements often appear describing in glowing terms the virtues of the litter. Never be seduced by words. When viewing the litter also look at the parents, the pedigree and the experience of the breeder who may be a complete newcomer to the breed and possessed of optimism not omniscience. It is certainly surprising that inexperienced owners feel able to assert they have show specimens in their litters. Maybe they have, but very often they have not!

The Litter

Whether you want a show prospect, a companion puppy or a potential worker, there are several points to look for when viewing the litter: the suitability and cleanliness of the environment; the condition of mother and puppies; and the temperament of mother and puppies. All should be sparkling clean - kennel accommodation and stock. Whilst some bitches lose weight after maternal duties, others do not, but most look a bit 'draggy' underneath. That is to be expected.

The author's Blackforest 'C' litter at 7½ weeks.

Nevertheless they should still look clean with a shining coat and be bright and alert – as should the puppies. They should not be fat, 'butterballs', to use an American expression, nor should they be too thin, like plucked chickens. A puppy should feel nicely covered to the touch and the coat should be clean and not have bits of stale food or excrement adhering to it. If they are not clean I should entertain serious doubts about hygiene and management in general. If puppies appear dirty when visitors come, what on earth are they (and the kennel accommodation) like when no-one is due to visit?

To look at a well-reared, healthy litter in clean surroundings is a pleasure, and it is often described by caring breeders for the nicest of reasons as 'time-wasters'. They spend hours watching the puppies playing, eating, sleeping and growing up because to have a litter is a rewarding event and never loses its fascination for the true animal lover. That is, someone who is concerned with all-round quality and not merely the money each little warm furry body represents.

Items to be Given to the New Owner

Signed pedigree.

Kennel Club Registration card (if this is through).

Diet Sheet (preferably this should be sent beforehand to enable

Happiness is a well-fed puppy.

food to be purchased).

Instructions on the breed (for first-time owners).

Dates of wormings carried out.

Signed inoculation certificates as appropriate.

The New Puppy's Requirements

A sleeping place (box, basket, crate) in a warm, draught-free area.

Metal food bowl.

Metal water bowl.

Leather collar with address/telephone number tag (a legal requirement when a dog is out in a public place). Note – several collars of increasing size will be required as the puppy grows.

Leather or nylon lead (not a chain lead with a leather handpiece).

Toys – rubber toys made specially for dogs (buy the largest size of ball, the solid rubber variety, to prevent asphyxiation through swallowing; but I don't allow a dog over 5 months to play with a ball because of this danger), cooked marrow bone stripped of flesh.

A secure back garden so that the puppy cannot wander off (or be stolen, as has happened not infrequently in urban areas).

A word of warning: do not under any circumstances buy a puppy which is under seven weeks old. Up to this time the puppy is still interacting and learning from its litter-mates. If taken to its new home

Two adorable pups from a litter by Madason the Graduate and Bellinas Wulfilia Germania.

before the seventh week, it may well become too fixated on human beings and be aggressive later on with other dogs. From the eighth week to the twelfth week, the puppy enters the fear period when a move to a new home is much more stressful, so try to have the puppy as near to the 49th day as possible. Instead of having a young puppy straight from the nest, some people prefer to have an older puppy or a young dog which has passed through the chewing, several meals a day, house-training stage. There are both advantages and disadvantages to this. The advantages are that its appearance and character are quite readily discernible and in dogs over one year the hip status can be confirmed. However, it is very necessary that the potential owner finds out as much as possible about the dog's previous history: the extent of socialisation and training and, above all with the older dog, whether it has any behavioural quirks which may pose problems in the future. It is not always easy to take on an older Rottweiler male; rarely is the new owner presented with the 'complete' dog, and careful, sympathetic handling as well as considerable patience may be required during the settling-in period. Should an older dog come from a kennel environment, it may well be that although it has received a certain amount of socialisation, it has had little in the way of mental stimulation and is not accustomed to the things that the average pet dog takes for granted – the busy urban scene, young children, loud noises, going out for walks in the twilight or dark, playing, chasing balls, etc. It may also be that its 'vocabulary' is very limited and words such as walk, ball, biscuit, dinner, etc. mean absolutely nothing to it. Such a dog may be thought rather stupid but dogs never stop learning and it is for the new owner to introduce it to a variety of new experiences and words. Do not expect an overnight conversion job – kennel dog into house pet – but the learning process can be mutually rewarding for both dog and owner.

Whatever the origin of the older dog, novice owners should not take on one which has aggressive tendencies. The novice owner is unlikely to have the expertise, the time, or the patience needed to sort out the problems of such a dog – given that they can be sorted out.

6 Caring for your Rottweiler

Feeding

Large breeds like the Rottweiler have a great deal of growing to do in a short time, so the amount and type of food is critical to correct development. A dog requires over forty nutrients in order to function properly, and the factors influencing energy requirements are: weight, activity, age, ambient temperature, individual nature of the animal and breeding/working status.

All-in-one or complete diets are preferred by some owners, while others give raw or cooked meat (and for puppies also milk and eggs) supplementing with biscuit, vitamins and minerals. Supplements are not required with complete diets. For a meat diet there are many good commercial preparations available which should be given strictly in accordance with the manufacturer's instructions. My own preference is for SA37 and sterilised boneflour. To ensure good bone formation, calcium and phosphorus, in the correct ratio, are essential.

Probably the most common errors made by the novice and sometimes even the quite experienced owner or breeder are with feeding: too much vitamin/mineral supplementation is given in the mistaken belief that if a little is good, more is even better. This can be most harmful to the puppy (see illustration). This dog was fed a complete diet and, in addition, was given one tablespoonful of cod liver oil per day. Unfortunately, he was not seen by a clinician until the condition had become irreversible and he had to be put down. *When* cod liver oil is necessary, the amount given should not exceed 1–2 *drops*.

Another not uncommon misconception is that an all-meat diet meets the needs of the growing puppy. Dogs are not carnivores as is often thought but omnivores. They need carbohydrate, too. The ratio of meat to carbohydrate in their diet should be around 50:50. Sometimes tripe is the only meat given and such a diet can result in poor, under-nourished stock. If unsupplemented or improperly supplemented, an all-meat diet can cause bone and joint deformities due to improper calcium and phosphorus metabolism. If a puppy is fed too high a proportion of meat in its diet, it may refuse the essential carbohydrates which it begins to find much less palatable.

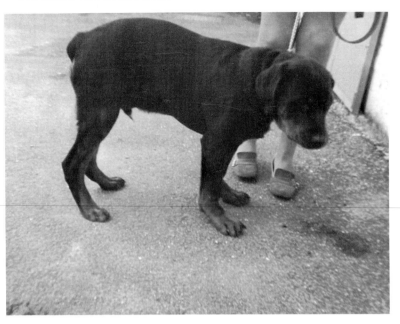

The sad result of the wrong type of feeding. This poor dog had to be put down.

Initially, your puppy should be given four or five meals a day; two or three meat and two milk for those on a 'natural' (i.e. not complete) diet. These should be reduced to three meals at around the age of three to four months and two at ten to twelve months. However, each puppy must be treated as an individual as there are exceptions which may need more frequent, smaller meals. I am utterly opposed to the practice of feeding young growing puppies for six days of the week and starving them on the seventh. To do this with growing youngsters can be harmful. Puppies are frequently fed for maximum growth which is a great mistake since this places an enormous strain on immature joints and ligaments which can lead to permanent damage. Informed opinion now advocates that the best course is to feed conservatively, ensuring that development takes place over a longer period. This results in less strain. So while the 'slimline' puppy may not look as attractive as the big overweight roly-poly, the chances are that it is set for an infinitely sounder life.

Feed an adult dog two meals a day. This practice has the advantage of not overloading the dog's stomach and enabling the meat and carbohydrate components of the diet to be fed separately. Such a regime is advocated by many specialists as it is thought that too full a stomach and mixing meat and biscuit together may contribute to the condition known as bloat.

Most Rottweilers, puppies and adults alike, have extremely good appetites, but occasionally one does come across a finicky eater. It is advisable to have the puppy or dog checked by your vet as this problem may be due to a number of factors. Difficult feeders cause much worry to their owners and, after the initial check up, if no problem is found, patience is advised. Try tempting the dog with different types of food or if possible, have another dog around which eats heartily. A last resort is hand-feeding: the problem here is that the puppy or adult may decide it likes all the attention and expects it to continue! There also seems to be some evidence that being a difficult eater may be inherited.

Points to Remember about Feeding
1. Feeding is one of life's great pleasures for the puppy and adult and it should be distraction-free, without adults or children interfering, teasing or fussing round.
2. It is not possible to lay down exact quantities of food which should be given. The owner must be guided by the condition and individual needs of the dog with working, convalescent, breeding, and lactating bitches as well as growing puppies requiring more nutrients.
3. Food should be kept under hygienic conditions and not be contaminated by flies, etc. It should be fed at room temperature (not straight from the refrigerator), and leftovers never kept for another meal.
4. Food which is 'off' should never be given.
5. Fix on feeding times and try to keep to them.
6. Dishes should be kept scrupulously clean; stainless steel ones are the best and, although expensive initially, they do last.
7. Any change in diet should be introduced gradually to avoid gastric upsets.
8. Dogs should not be exercised or worked within about one hour before or after a meal.
9. Fresh water should be available at all times. Some people think that the dog should not be allowed to drink immediately before or after a meal.
A great deal of research has been carried out into the effects of malnutrition in animals, and as long ago as 1920 it was discovered that undernutrition imposed during postnatal life in the rat results both in permanent growth stunting of total body weight and of brain weight (Jackson and Stewart 1920). Learning performance in rats was affected through malnutrition which continued into the next generation which was well fed. A researcher in 1975 stated that there is ample evidence and also general agreement that the malnourished individual (human as well as animal) differs qualitatively from the normally nourished one. He adapts in a different way to new environ-

ments, displays social interactions other than normal and shows different spontaneous behaviour under constant or changing environments.

Exercise

As with feeding, opinions differ as to exactly what exercise Rottweiler puppies and adults need. Certainly for puppies it is impossible to overestimate the importance of supervising activities during the first few months of life.

In the nest, from the time puppies are on their feet until they leave for their new homes at seven or eight weeks, exercise is found in their play with each other. The situation in the new home is very different. If other dogs are kept, the greatest care must be taken to ensure that the new puppy is not knocked about in rough company with the adults or even other puppies, as this can be extremely harmful. Nor should young children be allowed to drag or pull the puppy around. Young, heavy puppies should not be allowed to play roughly on hard surfaces like concrete, run up and down steps or stairs and jump into or out of cars. Supervision involves time and effort, and it is well worthwhile investing in the crate (or indoor kennel) mentioned in Chapter 8 for your growing, heavy puppy so that he can be put away for periods of rest after intensive play activity.

Rottweiler puppies should not be taken for formal walks until they are about five months old. The exception is walks down the high street (after inoculations have been completed) to gain social experience which it is essential for them to receive at a young age. If there is a *good* training club in your area which runs puppy classes, take your puppy there to accustom him to other dogs in a controlled situation.

Lead training can be started in the house and then in the garden so that when formal walks on the lead begin, the puppy is already trained not to pull. Walking distance may be increased gradually until by the age of a year, the dog can be walking two to three miles. Short periods of free running can be permitted from the age of nine to ten months as this exercise is good for lung and muscle development.

To bring a dog to peak muscular condition try exercising him at a trot while you ride a bicycle. However, this should not be started until he is a year or more old. At any age, the amount of exercise depends on the dog being sound. Activities should be restricted if he is lame, and particular care should be taken when exercising heavy, fast-growing puppies.

Dogs which are to be trained to jump should not start training until they are 18 months old and then they must be fit and well muscled.

Housing Conditions

Housing requirements are basically the same for all dogs. Their quarters should be damp- and draught-proof with a raised bed of some sort with a blanket, Vetbed (or similar). Some establishments use straw or sawdust for dogs kept in kennels. House dogs need a place where they can retire to sleep or rest away from human attention and there are many excellent types of dog beds and baskets on the market.

Whether kept in the house or kennel remember that Rottweilers can tolerate the cold better than heat. Indeed the breed is very susceptible to hot sunshine and there should always be shade available in warm weather. Should Rottweilers be required to work under hot conditions, it should be for short periods only initially. Time can be increased as they acclimatise.

Never leave a slip-type collar or chain on a puppy or adult in the house or kennel, use only a buckle-type as the former can become caught in objects and cause strangulation.

Teething

This is a time of stress for the puppy. The first or milk teeth start to fall out from the twelfth week onwards when the permanent teeth should begin to appear. The owner should examine the mouth from time to time to check that none of the milk teeth remain in position which causes the new teeth to be out of alignment. If this happens they may need to be removed by a vet. It can be helpful if the puppy is given a hard rubber toy to chew on, but playing tug-of-war games is not recommended as the occlusion of the teeth (the bite) may be adversely affected. At this time the intake of calcium and phosphorus must be monitored, and if the puppy appears to be down on his pasterns he may need to have extra calcium, possibly by injection. This should be discussed with your vet.

A dog's teeth are usually healthy and decay is not a problem. Tartar should not be allowed to accumulate as this can cause bad breath and gum disease. Giving a large marrow bone at regular intervals helps as do various commercial preparations. Scaling may be carried out by your vet. Please note that marrow bones are the *only* type of bones which should be given to a dog.

Ears

During teething, ears, especially the desirable small ones, tend to be held incorrectly with a crease in the centre; they 'fly'. Massaging them into the correct position usually rights this, but not overnight, so patience and application are required. Gently massage the ears several times a day as follows.

Have the puppy sitting down in front of you. Carefully place the index finger into the opening of the ear, then with the ear between the thumb and index finger, massage it gently but firmly with the thumb, beginning at the junction of ear and skull and moving towards the extremities. In this way the crease is removed and circulation promoted. If, after some weeks there is no improvement, consult your vet about sticking the ear down in the correct position. When this is done, it has to be 'unstuck' every few days so that the ears can receive ventilation and infection is avoided. Healthy ears do not smell, are cool to the touch, do not look inflamed and do not have a brownish discharge in them. It is a good idea to examine the ears every week. Do not poke down them with a finger or some sharp object, use cotton buds. If there is any discharge check with your vet what remedy to use. The ear is a delicate mechanism and Do-It-Yourself potions are not advised.

Eyes
Eye problems are dealt with in Chapter 7. Any excessive watering or inflammation of the conjunctiva (the white part surrounding the eye) should be checked by your vet as symptoms may be caused by a variety of factors: ulcers, blocked tear ducts, etc. Again, DIY remedies are not recommended.

Coat
Whatever the texture of a Rottweiler's coat, it should be clean and glossy. To achieve this, daily grooming, correct feeding and good health (e.g. freedom from internal parasites) are prerequisites. The short coat makes grooming a minor chore, and if the dog is accustomed to being brushed from puppyhood, there should be no resentment on his part; instead, most dogs enjoy the attention. Some owners with vacuum cleaners which have attachments actually 'brush' their dogs with these. Again, the dog must be gradually introduced to this form of grooming. Other methods are a steel 'rake' comb drawn gently through the coat with a soft dandy brush to finish off, or a hound glove, or rubber brush. A short-coated breed like the Rottweiler hardly ever needs bathing in a temperate climate if given regular grooming. While losing hair and sometimes for a short while after the moult has finished, the coat may be rather scurfy. Continue regular grooming and the scurf will disappear.

Nails
Not all Rottweilers have the desired short-toed, tight feet and this, as well as insufficient exercise on hard surfaces, necessitates clipping or filing the nails. If this is not carried out, the length of the nails causes

the toes to spread, making them more vulnerable to injury.

I have never met a Rottweiler which really liked having a pedicure, and there are owners who are unwilling or even afraid to cut nails because their dogs have threatened or actually bitten them, or because they were concerned about taking off too much nail, so injuring the quick. This means that the dog lumbers around with overlong nails

This is a good position for grooming adult dogs, but not growing puppies.

Carefully filing the nails.

and eventually is in some discomfort. Or he is taken to the vet for attention and may need to be given a general anaesthetic. This is expensive and unnecessary if the puppy is gently introduced to clipping or filing. My own preference is for filing.

Use a large file such as a carpenter's, support the dog's toe against your finger and gently file in one direction until a small area of grey appears in the centre of the nail; proceed with caution for a few more strokes until the grey area disappears and becomes dark and shiny. Stop at that point. It may be that the dog will show signs of discomfort before this if it is sensitive, in which case stop there. While filing takes longer than clipping, it is worthwhile as the dogs seem much happier with this procedure. Young puppies have thin nails which can be clipped. It only takes a second to do each nail and just the tip should be removed.

Inoculations

The diseases against which a dog is generally inoculated are distemper, hardpad, hepatitis, leptospirosis and parvovirus. Parvovirus is of comparatively recent origin and research is still being carried on into the best regime of inoculations against it. Puppies need to be inoculated before they are taken out and about with additional parvovirus injections being given as necessary. (A blood test is useful here.) Adults should be boosted annually and your vet will advise you of what is required.

Correctly filed nail.

Worming
The breeder should already have wormed a puppy one or more times and given the new owner a note of the dates so the puppy need only be given follow-up doses. Thereafter worming should be routinely done at three-monthly intervals and the appropriate medication obtained from the vet. Additional worming should be carried out after any flea infestation.

The Older Dog
Large dogs do not live as long as small ones and the lifespan of the Rottweiler is around ten years. The oldest Rottweiler I have seen was a big Dutch dog who achieved fifteen summers and I managed to keep one bitch until she was within one week of her fourteenth birthday. There is some evidence that longevity runs in lines and Rottweilers living in a hot climate do not seem to have such a long lifespan as those who live in more temperate climates.

Mrs Feldmann's lovely old dog Bellinas Hasso at his 13th birthday party.

A Rottweiler should never be permitted to become fat. Some specimens seen, even in the show ring, bear a remarkable resemblance to waddling puddings. This is not conducive to health or activity. As a dog ages he will need less food (but always good food) and more attention paid to keeping him fit.

Older animals should be watched carefully to see that there are no irregular discharges from prepuce (dog) or vagina (bitch) and any lumps on the body or legs should be checked immediately. If the dog is off-colour for more than a day, take him for a veterinary examination. Older dogs sleep more, are less excitable and give a great deal of pleasure: they know your ways and you theirs.

Your Veterinary Surgeon

One of the more important choices in any dog owner's life is that of choosing your vet. Unless you live in an isolated, country area, it is likely there will be more than one practice within reasonable distance. Check them out. Ascertain whether Rottweilers are loved or loathed.

Consider the vets themselves: in the main are their personalities compatible with your own? Are they willing to permit owner participation, e.g. if a general anaesthetic is required, will you be allowed to stay to reassure your dog while it is given its premed? And do they keep you totally informed? Are they willing to refer to a consultant if necessary? If the response to these questions is positive, then you may have found the ideal vet for your Rottweiler. Even otherwise friendly Rottweilers do not always like having a routine veterinary examination and their reactions are different from those you might expect from, say, a gundog breed. This should be understood and allowed for by the veterinary surgeon. We have found that even among the most eminent vets there is an unfortunate tendency to measure temperament on one dimension only, 'handleability'. If a dog does not submit with passivity to an examination, then its temperament is dismissed as bad. This is as surprising as it is sad; sad because in this way a breed can be branded as bad tempered or vicious when all that is required is an understanding of how Rottweilers behave and that the presence of owners, whenever possible, during examination or treatment is infinitely reassuring and contributes to reducing any stress the dog may suffer.

So take the greatest care in choosing your vet and while it is unlikely you can make visits to him actually pleasurable for your dog, I do emphasise that it is the owner's responsibility to teach him the way to behave and the necessity of submitting to routine inoculations and examinations. One of my own dogs, the late Ch. Horst from Blackforest CDex, a real toughie, adored my vet and would rush into the surgery off lead for his welcoming biscuit and, having had that, would allow the examination or inoculation and then expect another biscuit as a reward. If your vet will co-operate in giving titbits, before and after dealing with your dog then your dog may well view future visits to the vet in a more favourable light. Some dogs do need to be restrained; it is only fair not to put the vet at risk so something like a pyjama cord should be tied firmly round the muzzle and then round the dog's neck.

Treatment can be expensive but there are now very satisfactory insurance schemes whereby your dog may be insured for the greater part of the cost. It is well worth taking out an insurance as soon as you get your puppy.

A dog showing any of the following signs should be checked by a veterinary surgeon.
1. Abnormal behaviour – sudden viciousness or lethargy.
2. Abnormal discharges from the nose, eyes or other body openings.
3. Abnormal lumps, limping or difficulty getting up or lying down.
4. Loss of appetite, marked weight losses or gains, excessive water

consumption. Difficult, abnormal or uncontrolled waste elimination.
5. Excessive head shaking, scratching and licking or biting any part of the body.
6. Dandruff, loss of hair, open sores and a ragged or dull coat. Foul breath or excessive tartar deposits on teeth.

Veterinary Homeopathy

A few vets in the UK use homeopathic remedies in addition to conventional treatment and those Rottweiler owners who have used them have found that generally their dogs derive much benefit. Essentially, homeopathy is a natural healing process with three basic principles.
1. A medicine which in large doses produces symptoms of a disease will in small doses cure that disease.
2. By extreme dilution, the medicine's curative properties are enhanced and all the poisonous or undesirable side-effects are lost.
3. Homeopathic medicines are prescribed individually by the study of the whole person/animal.
Sixty percent of homeopathic remedies come from plant sources and a wide range is available. They look exactly like other medicines and may be in the form of tablets, granules, ointments, liquids or suppositories.

Six remedies in common use, some of which I have used with success are:
Arnica for bruising, sprains and swelling, shock before and after operations. For after-effects of tooth extraction.
Caudophyllum given in the later stages of pregnancy; birth complications and stress of pups reduced.
Calendula lotion for bathing wounds, sores, etc.
Apis Mel. for insect bites and stings and any injury where there is swelling containing fluid.
Rhus tox. for conditions of rheumatism and arthritis which are worse after rest but which improve after exercise.
Hypericum is useful as a pain killer, e.g. bruising of bones or nerves, for lacerated wounds and deep puncture bites, and after operations.
And there are many, many other remedies. A list of vets who use homeopathic remedies may be obtained from the British Association of Homeopathic Veterinary Surgeons, 19A Cavendish Square, London W1M 9AD.

7 Hereditary and other Health Problems

Distemper, Hardpad, Leptospirosis, Hepatitis and Parvovirus

All these are killer diseases. It is essential that puppies are inoculated against them and that adults receive boosters throughout their lives. New owners should be given a certificate by the breeder, signed by a veterinary surgeon, showing what injections have been given, with dates. Thereafter a regime of inoculations approved by the individual vet should be followed.

Since parvovirus is such a new disease, research is still being carried out and many questions remain unanswered. It seems that maternal antibodies may persist in Rottweiler puppies for longer than in the majority of other breeds and so interfere with inoculations against the disease if they are given too early. However, one school of thought maintains that by giving inoculations early the puppy's immune system may be 'primed' for future injections. But much remains to be discovered about this highly contagious and distressing disease which has claimed the lives of so many Rottweilers of all ages. Your vet should be aware of the latest position concerning timing of inoculations, so keep in close touch with him. At present, many owners and breeders have their puppies and brood bitches blood tested to see whether they have an acceptable level of immunity, and this is a good idea. In the case of brood bitches, this should be done before mating.

Listlessness, runny eyes and nose, sickness and bloody, foul-smelling diarrhoea are all signs which require an *immediate* check by the vet. Do not delay an instant.

Cystitis/Vaginitis

These are conditions which sometimes affect bitches, both puppies and adults. The former is characterised by very frequent passing of urine and sometimes straining without passing any; the latter is a sticky discharge of pus. Medication from the vet is necessary together with a clean, stress-free environment and a constant supply of fresh drinking water.

Ear Problems

Indicated by shaking of the head or rubbing head along the ground. These can be due to ear mites or infection. Some Rottweilers have narrow ear channels which make infections more difficult to treat. A veterinary check is required in order that the correct drug is prescribed.

Eye Problems

Runny eyes may be due to a variety of causes, such as blocked tear ducts, conjunctivitis, ulcers, entropion (eyelids turning inwards) or trichiasis (eyelashes growing inwards and irritating the eye).

Entropion is a hereditary disease but the exact mode of inheritance is unknown. It may be manifested in puppies from the age of about six weeks but the condition may right itself when the skull has developed, although it is not always so. Mild entropion may be dealt with by using an ointment as directed by the vet, but severe cases require an operation. This should not be delayed because to have skin or hair rubbing against the eye is extremely painful for the dog who will rub his eyes which exacerbates the condition. Apart from the cruelty aspect, if left untreated, the pressure on the cornea causes ulcers which, in turn, eventually cause blindness. This remedial operation, whereby excess skin is taken away, is one which can be very successful. I say can, because some vets take away too much skin and the dog looks as if it has been operated on with a knife and fork! It is often better to have two operations so that the correct amount of skin is eventually removed. Try to find out if your vet has experience of this type of surgery, or go to a consultant ophthalmologist.

Ectropion is also seen occasionally in the breed when the eyelid is loose and turns outwards, so allowing dust and debris to collect. Again this is a painful condition and can be helped by surgery.

Orthopaedic Conditions

As a large breed, the Rottweiler is more prone to this sort of problem than smaller breeds.

1. HIP DYSPLASIA

Hip dysplasia is a malformation of the hip joint (ball-and-socket) which in its most severe form causes great pain, crippling and possibly means the dog will have to be put down.

There is no way of ensuring that a mating will produce a litter with sound hips, but research has shown beyond a doubt that there is a much greater likelihood of sound hips if both parents and as many as possible of the forebears have good hips themselves, since this disease is inherited.

The only way of reducing the incidence is by selective breeding from animals with good hip joint conformation. To determine the hip status, the dog should be X-rayed at any time after it reaches the age of one, unless of course it has been persistently lame before this. The X-rays, on which the dog's Kennel Club number has been put at the time of X-raying, should be submitted to the British Veterinary Association/Kennel Club Hip Scoring Scheme. The great advantage of this scheme is that a panel of vets, each with a specialist knowledge in this field, evaluate the plates, so ensuring a uniform standard of interpretation. This is an absolute requirement if the overall standard within a breed is to be assessed and the conclusion reached as to which animals should not be used for breeding.

In a breed which is not numerically strong, it may be necessary to breed from animals which have less than the desired standard of hips. In Rottweilers this is no longer necessary.

The degree of abnormality of the joint varies from complete dislocation to one which has borderline changes only which do not affect the dog functionally. In severe cases, lameness may start at a few months old, and the puppy may experience difficulty in getting up from a recumbent position. He may walk with a very stiff gait with the weight taken mainly by the forehand, or exhibit an odd 'bunny-hopping' gait, an inability to sustain the strains of exercise, and lack of musculature in the hindquarters, giving the flanks and upper thighs a flat, poor look.

Many cases improve with age when the muscles become fully developed and with careful management by the owner in not allowing the youngster to become overweight and restricting exercise. Arthritic changes over time may cause problems as the dog ages, but each case must be assessed on its merits in order that the appropriate treatment may be given. The degree of dysplasia revealed by X-raying is by no means always reflected in the dog's mobility.

Various surgical procedures are available, including complete hip replacement, when an operation is deemed to be necessary.

The fact that a Rottweiler suffers mild or even moderate hip dysplasia does not mean that it will not make a perfectly satisfactory pet. While it should not be used for breeding, by carefully controlling its diet to keep it slim and by not exercising it beyond its capabilities, it should be able to lead a fairly normal life.

Dogs which move with drive and power must not be assumed to have good hips and that is why all dogs used for breeding should have their hips X-rayed.

2. OSTEOCHONDROSIS
This term is used to describe a general condition the dog has. It is not thought to be injury-induced, but due to a developmental error

in cartilage and bone during puppyhood. Fragments sometimes drop off into the joint capsule. Four different joints may be affected: shoulder, elbow, stifle and hock.

In recent years, with the greatly increased numbers born, problems of forehand lameness have been seen more frequently. Unfortunately, insufficient research has been undertaken for it to be concluded that these problems are inherited. J. Grondalen (1981), a Norwegian veterinary clinician, has investigated the condition and found Rottweilers to be particularly prone to elbow lameness, males more so than females in the ratio 2:1, although shoulder lesions are also found.

All cases of lameness should be rested and if the condition persists for more than a few days the dog should be examined by a vet without delay in order that any treatment may be started and the joint not damaged further by excessive use. Should an operation be required, my preference is for it to be carried out at a university department.

3. RUPTURED CRUCIATE LIGAMENT

These are the ligaments which hold the stifle (knee) joint firm, and although they are extremely strong, a sudden twist such as the dog's foot slipping into a rut when running at speed, can cause a rupture. Severe lameness of sudden onset in a hind leg should be checked out immediately by a vet. Ruptured cruciate ligaments can be repaired surgically very successfully, using a variety of techniques, but the ultimate outcome is dependent on two other factors apart from the surgeon's skill. Firstly, the delay between the rupture and the operation being performed, as any arthritic changes which have taken place cannot be reversed by the operation and secondly, a carefully supervised convalescence. During the first four weeks the dog goes outside into the garden *on a lead* to relieve itself and comes straight in again. For a further month very slow, steady and *short* walks of 50–100 yards to start with, and then for another month increasing exercise on the lead and short periods of free exercise, with no romping with other dogs or rough-housing.

Research is being undertaken at the present time into this problem by a veterinary team at the University of Liverpool, which indicates that there may be a 'new' syndrome appearing in young dogs (less than three years old) in the large heavy breeds, including the Rottweiler. It is characterised by premature stretching of the cranial cruciate ligament which eventually ruptures. The stretching of the ligament is associated with inflammatory changes (osteoarthritis) which worsen considerably once the ligament has been completely ruptured. This problem is causing concern because there appears to be an increase in the incidence and it is affecting such young dogs. Many of these can be diagnosed as early as one year and this can result in their going lame and being affected with joint problems for the rest of their lives. Attempts will be made to establish whether there is a primary defect in the ligament itself or whether there is a generalised joint disease of which cruciate pathology forms a part.

Skin Conditions

FOLLICULAR OR DEMODECTIC MANGE

Characterised by loss of hair in patches without irritation, first on the head, around eyes and nose and on or near feet. Treatment is not easy and prompt veterinary attention is essential. Elimination of stress plays an important part in the treatment.

SARCOPTIC MANGE

Symptoms of this are patchy loss of hair, generally starting from the muzzle and moving backwards often on ear flaps or legs, with small pustules forming which cause intense irritation, making the dog scratch violently. Shaving of affected areas and dipping are usual treatments but the vet must be consulted immediately.

CHEYLETIELLA

Resembles flaky scurf and is easy to see on black-and-tan dogs like Rottweilers. Mostly occurs on the posterior surface of the back and gives rise to itching. Consult vet without delay.

ECZEMA

Some dogs are allergic to things in the natural environment like certain plants and fleas. The presence of even one flea, or its droppings, can cause a reaction–inflammation, tremendous irritation (eczema) and twitching of the skin on the back. Elimination of fleas, using one of the proprietary products plus one or two antihistamine injections as directed by the vet should clear this up. Fleas breed off the dog and flea allergy can cause very real distress so veterinary advice should be sought straight away.

Moist eczema sometimes develops from an allergy when scratching damages the skin, resulting in a sticky discharge which mats the hair. Rottweilers seem to be quite prone to this, and since it causes great discomfort because of the intense irritation, prompt attention is necessary. The matted hairs should be cut away carefully, the area gently cleaned with a saline solution (1 level teaspoonful of salt dissolved in boiling water which is allowed to cool) and then dressed with an ointment or powder. If left untreated, these 'wet' patches spread very quickly, causing great discomfort to the dog.

Professional advice should always be sought in the case of skin conditions as diagnosis of some types may require a skin scraping and each needs individual treatment. Tests may also need to be carried out to determine the substance that the dog is allergic to, and in certain skin diseases a change of diet forms part of the treatment.

Bloat and Gastric Torsion

This is a very serious condition, also seen in other animals like cows and horses, in which the stomach becomes distended and sometimes twisted, the cause being a digestive problem. At the first sign of swelling of the stomach the dog should be taken to the vet. Minutes can be vital if the dog's life is to be saved.

The condition is most often seen in the heavy-bodied breeds and Rottweilers are known to have succumbed to it. Research into the cause continues. As precautions, it is better to feed twice a day so as not to overload the stomach; not to feed unsoaked meal; not to mix meat and meal and not to feed before or after exercise.

This condition is a killer and *immediate* veterinary attention is critical.

Cancer

This is a major cause of death amongst Rottweilers, the most common areas of cancer being the long bones, mammary glands in bitches and prostate in dogs. Operations can be carried out in some cases as well as radio and chemotherapy, but radiotherapy is available only at university departments. Limb amputations in the case of bone cancer have been done with limited success. Here, the consideration must be the size and age of the animal as well as the advice of the vet and inclinations of the owner.

Over-eating

There is no doubt that the majority of Rottweilers are greatly addicted to the food dish and appear to have a never-ending desire for 'grub'. Some put on weight with an exceedingly small intake, while others require a much larger amount in order to keep in condition. The quantity of food should be so regulated that the dog does not look like some perambulating pudding. As a rough guide, you should be able to feel (not see!) the dog's ribs; they should not be upholstered by a cushion of fat and there should be a clearly-defined waist. Owners do a great disservice to their dogs by allowing them to put on weight and their general health and activity suffer in the process. There are some extremely fat Rottweilers around and one can only advise a consultation with the vet to work out a balanced diet which may include a well-known tinned obesity diet.

Just as too much weight should be avoided, so should too little, and a dog whose ribs and pin bones are clearly visible should have its food intake increased, possibly to three meals a day and, if required, a veterinary check should be made. To reduce a Rottweiler to emaciated proportions in the mistaken belief that it produces a hard, working condition is totally misguided and stupid. If one finds it necessary to take off so much weight in order to jump the dog in trials, then it is highly questionable that it should be jumped at all.

Pancreatic Insufficiency

This is a problem not infrequently encountered in Rottweilers and is manifested by loss of weight or inability to put on weight, with pale, fatty, loose stools. The dog is unable to produce a sufficient quantity of the enzyme trypsin from the pancreas but the condition can normally be controlled by medication and veterinary advice is necessary in order to decide on the dose required and whether any change of diet is needed. Thin Rottweilers, apparently over-eating, should have a faecal test done as the condition is often exacerbated by delay. It is sometimes associated with sugar diabetes which would also make the dog thin with a poor coat and even when treatment is being carried out the condition needs to be monitored occasionally.

Kidney Disease

Older dogs, especially males, are more prone to some ailments like kidney disease. Any sudden loss of weight or pronounced increase of water intake should be checked promptly and treated, otherwise kidney conditions become acute. Sufferers may need to be put on a special tinned food which is low in protein and is obtainable from vets.

Poisons

If you think your dog has swallowed a poisonous substance contact your vet without delay. In the case of rare or obscure poisons your vet may care to contact the Toxicology Hotline at the University of Illinois, U.S.A. which is open 24 hours a day. The number is 010.1.217.333.3611.

These are some of the more common problems encountered in Rottweilers. The time-worn adage 'A stitch in time saves nine' can never be more true than with dogs. If you think there is anything wrong, have your vet examine the dog without delay. It is far better to be overcautious. But be fair to your vet: don't look at your dog all day wondering whether to ask for a home visit, and then decide in the small hours that you better had!

8　Basic Training

Developmental Stages

Largely unnoticed in England by breeders and the dog-owning public, the book *New Knowledge of Dog Behaviour* by the American Clarence Pfaffenberger, offered new insights into the developmental stages of puppies which not only had application to the selection and training of guide dogs for the blind with which the author was primarily concerned, but also to the socialisation and integration into the family of the companion dog. Even now, almost two decades after publication, these findings are still not widely known or used for the benefit of dog and owner. Socialisation is the sensible, sympathetic and gradual introduction of the puppy to sights, sounds, smells and human beings which together and individually make up the world in which it has to live. Remember that a dog's life revolves mainly around its sense of smell. While it is important for all breeds of dog to be adequately socialised as puppies, it is vital that the large guarding breeds, like the Rottweiler, are properly introduced to the complex world of people and objects. It seems that there may well be a difference between breeds as to the amount of socialisation necessary for optimum development and in general Rottweilers need a large amount. Puppies which, through the ignorance, laziness or indifference of their owners, are prevented from mixing with people and becoming accustomed to sights and sounds of town and country grow up without the confidence to deal with new situations and people. This means they can be nervous, suspicious and even fear-biters, uneasy and unhappy away from their own territory, pale shadows of the dogs they might have become.

So an understanding of the stages a puppy goes through are of inestimable value to all who want to get the best from their puppy as an adult.

1. INITIAL PERIOD 1ST–7TH WEEK INCLUSIVE

This is from the 1st to 49th day, during which time the puppy should remain with his dam and litter-mates. From 1st to 20th day, the puppy's needs are purely physical – food, sleep, warmth and his mother. Real learning does not take place and the puppy is neuro-logically very primitive. From 21st–49th day, rapid neurological development occurs and puppies learn to become dogs – playing, vocalising, biting and seeing what effects these activities have on their mother and siblings, as well as learning to accept discipline from their mother. Removal from the litter should not take place during this period. If they are removed these puppies tend to find it difficult to relate to other dogs and they may be aggressive, difficult to breed and less responsive to training.

2. SOCIALISATION PERIOD 7TH–12TH WEEK

Research has shown that the best time for a puppy to go to his new home is during the 7th week, when his brain is neurologically com-plete and he is able to learn whatever an adult dog can learn, although of course he can concentrate for only short periods and is limited in what tasks he can do by his physical immaturity and stamina.

This is the time when the puppy should be introduced in a careful and sympathetic manner to as many sights and sounds of the world which will form part of his future life. For example, inside the home, the vacuum cleaner, radio and TV, and outside; town traffic as well as other animals, within the restrictions imposed by the immunisation regime. Time spent by the owner accustoming the puppy to all these things lays the best possible foundation for enabling the puppy to develop into a confident adult. Learning which takes place during this period is permanent and it is important that unintentional learning does not occur like cat chasing, getting up on chairs or beds, waiting for titbits at the meal table, etc.

3. FEAR PERIOD 8TH–11TH WEEK

It is now known that should a puppy suffer any frightening experi-ences during this period, they will have a permanent scarring effect. This is the time of maximum vulnerability. Stressful situations should be avoided as far as possible and visits to the vet for injections should be made more pleasant by taking along toys and titbits and by asking the vet to co-operate by making a fuss of the puppy. Elective surgery, e.g. hernia should be postponed until after this period.

4. DOMINANCE PERIOD 12TH–16TH WEEK

The puppy has been gaining confidence all the time and now begins to test his owner to see who is pack-leader, sometimes by attempting to mouth or bite the owner, albeit in a playful way, or biting and pulling the lead when out or during training. It is thought essential that such behaviour is firmly discouraged, but in no way should the puppy be 'flattened'. There should be no tugs of war after the puppy reaches the age of 13 weeks, nor wrestling or pitting of canine and human strengths. Men especially have an urge to do this and it is not always easy to convince the macho type that it is counter-productive!

Learning to mix with other animals is an important step in socialisation.

Serious training should begin now when seniority can easily be established by teaching the puppy a few simple commands like sit, down, stay, come. While the majority of dogs are probably not interested in becoming pack-leader, many Rottweiler males are, and for the owners of such dogs, this period is especially significant. It should be remembered that by the age of 16 weeks a puppy's emotions are set and, barring environmental accidents, he is what he will always be. You have the raw material but it can be mediated by training.

5. INDEPENDENCE PERIOD 4–8 months

Independence of thought and action characterise this period when the puppy turns a deaf ear to a command such as 'come' and goes smartly off in the opposite direction. Its duration is variable and the situation needs to be handled carefully so that the habit of 'doing his own thing' does not become fixed. Keep the puppy on a lead so that he cannot please himself and only let him off when you are sure he is trained and returns on command. Make haste slowly is a valuable maxim; it is not merely desirable but essential that a large and powerful dog like a Rottweiler is completely reliable in this respect. It can keep him (and you) out of trouble if he displays any inclination to chase other dogs, livestock, moving vehicles or even people.

6. SECOND FEAR PERIOD 6–14 MONTHS

Less well marked than the first period this usually lasts only a few weeks. During this time the young dog may suddenly appear apprehensive of both new and familiar objects. The best way to get through this is to be patient with the youngster and be confident. Talk quietly and calmly while continuing training, for training gives a dog self-confidence and it will solve just about every psychological dominance issue that will arise.

7. ADOLESCENCE TO MATURITY 1–4 YEARS

Adolescence occurs earlier in small breeds, later in large ones. When a dog has reached sexual maturity, it may well test for leadership again. Handle firmly, but kindly, and continue training so that the routine of discipline remains during this time.

Increasing aggression may also be displayed by the dog, house-callers being greeted by barking or growling when hitherto they were greeted as long-lost friends. And dogs which were friends now fight – or try to.

By no means every dog challenges the accepted order of things or displays any marked behavioural changes, but canine adolescence and its accompanying psychological changes should be familiar to an owner so that any adjustments may be made. It is during this time that problems have arisen with Rottweilers, mostly males, because owners are not aware of these changes. The dog challenges, the owner does not know how to cope and is frightened; and the dog takes over as pack-leader.

Should the dog exhibit any of these tendencies, keep calm and continue his training, establishing a regular routine so that control is continued and his response to basic commands is instantaneous. However, if you want reassurance or wish to talk over the dog's behaviour, don't hesitate to contact the breeder or a trainer who is experienced with Rottweilers.

These are the developmental stages (sequential and invariant) and guidelines have been given on how the owner should deal with each. Since this is not a manual of training, specific instructions are not given on how to teach individual exercises; for this see Appendix 1.

Common problems

Over the years it has become apparent, often painfully so, that the same problems crop up with regularity amongst the pet-owning Rottweiler public and even amongst breeders and show goers who have owned other breeds before. This is largely through ignorance of canine psychology and the strength of character of Rottweilers, especially the males.

Pet owners' problems can start with puppies of five or six months which are said to be 'out of control'; they growl, are extremely possessive over food or other objects and are not amenable to discipline. This is the time of testing and it is crucial for the owner to establish his leadership either by doing training exercises (sit, down, stay, etc.) at home and away from distractions like family or other pets, or by attending a suitable training class, or seeking private professional help. Such a situation does not resolve itself and swift positive action is required. It scarcely needs stressing that if this sort of behaviour continues unchecked, a dangerous dog is the result. If the local training class will not take a puppy under six months old then look further afield for one which does.

Another problem encountered is intolerance of strangers. As mentioned earlier, puppies need to be socialised with people of all ages, shapes and sizes, and shown that they are to be accepted. Mistakenly, some people who want their puppies to grow up into good guards, prevent them from meeting strangers or being touched by them; the only effect this has is to reduce the dog's confidence and self-reliance.

As they grow older, some dogs may resent the rather rough, over-familiar handling that some people unthinkingly give, under the false impression that dogs like to be patted vigorously. Commonsense indicates that the dog should not have to suffer the buffets of the over-enthusiastic, well-meaning ignoramus, which is where the careful owner should exert control of the situation. But, having said that, the dog must not be permitted to decide who can touch him and who cannot in everyday social encounters, and he must not be allowed to menace passers-by or behave unpredictably towards home visitors. It is up to the owner to teach the dog what is required and to protect him from the occasionally overwhelming embraces of adults and children alike. Dogs are not good at knowing what they should do; they are only good at knowing what we train them to do.

Some Rottweilers, again usually males, can be very aggressive towards other dogs, and it is as well to know of this propensity when acquiring a puppy. In this way it can be socialised towards other dogs (and other animals) from the time it arrives in its new home, and any show of aggression, barking, growling or lunging towards other dogs must be corrected at once. It is not enough to pull the puppy back from another dog, it must be told in no uncertain terms and tones that such behaviour is not acceptable. When the puppy has been checked, do not praise it, for it will associate the praise with the undesired conduct. The puppy must never be allowed to get away with bad behaviour like this, for while it is not difficult to stop it physically from lunging, it is a very different matter with a fully grown adult weighing upwards of 100 lbs.

Aggressive displays between exhibits, which may be seen in the show ring from time to time, often go unchecked because the handlers consider it makes the dogs stand on their toes and look better to the judge. Maybe it does, but it puts other exhibits at risk and can cause a chain reaction of aggression throughout the class. It also gives the worst impression of the breed to the public. It should be firmly discouraged by judges. Such dogs are a potential danger in the show ring and elsewhere. There is nothing smart about having an aggressive dog of any breed.

The Halti or head collar.

A fairly recent innovation in the way of equipment which assists those with dogs which pull or lunge, is the 'Halti'. This is a head collar for dogs, like a horse's halter except that it has a slip ring under the jaw and, by attaching the lead to this and raising one's arms, the noseband is tightened, the mouth is closed and the dog's head turned towards the handler. In this way the dog can be controlled without yanks on the check chain or by pulling to choking point on an ordinary collar. The owner has complete control without any pain or discomfort to the dog. It is useful for training and for pullers. Because a dog is not accustomed to wearing a noseband, the Halti should be introduced gradually in a stress-free situation (at home without other dogs or family present). Because it is quickly associated with going out, soon the dog cannot wait to have the Halti put on! This device deserves nothing but praise and it is to be hoped that the days of great jerks on the check chain, so uncomfortable and even injurious to the dog, will have gone forever.

Food/Object Possessiveness

Another irritating habit which can develop with any dog is being very possessive over food and objects; this behaviour, if left unchecked, is likely to cause problems when the dog is older. An adult Rottweiler baring its teeth in a snarl is an intimidating sight. Here again, the owner must intervene immediately the pup starts growling or showing his teeth. Tell him to 'Stop it' in a loud voice, remove the food bowl, and tell him to sit; praise him and give the food back again. This action should be repeated until the puppy accepts it, but in order that he will not become resentful of people approaching while he is eating, occasionally (or even frequently) approach him and, instead of taking the food bowl away, give him some more food. In this way, the puppy comes to realise that he will get the food back or have more food put into the bowl. Should he snap at first when the bowl is taken away, give him a sharp tap on the nose and say 'Stop it'.

The same strategy applies to possessiveness with articles; try to get him to bring it to you; if he does, praise lavishly, take it away from him and give a titbit. At first it may be necessary to give a titbit each time, but then give one occasionally so the puppy does not know when to expect it. This, known as intermittent reinforcement, is much more effective than rewarding continuously (continuous reinforcement). If the puppy will not bring the object to you, go up quietly and take it from him and then proceed as with food, sometimes taking the object away, sometimes giving him another.

Another problem is begging at the table; just do not start to feed at mealtimes and the habit will not develop.

Chewing

Occurs particularly during teething at five to six months and again at eight to nine months when the adult teeth are settling in. The puppy should be given his own toys and great care taken to keep attractive articles like shoes, gloves, scarves, etc. out of his reach. What you are doing is re-directing chewing activities to alternative and acceptable items. This is where a crate (see Crate Training p. 80) is most helpful as the puppy can be put in it when the owner is absent, thus preventing damage to carpets, chairs, table legs, etc.

House Training

House training is a subject about which there are still a lot of misunderstandings, some involving real cruelty. It is astounding that some still believe a puppy's nose should be rubbed in any mess it makes. I think it should be the owner's nose which is rubbed in it! By the time a puppy leaves for its new home at the age of 7 or 8 weeks, it does not have complete control of its bladder. The puppy should be put outside immediately on waking, after a meal, after playing and at regular intervals throughout the day; every hour or two at first. He should be taken to the same spot each time and given the same command like 'Be quick', 'Go on' etc. After he has obliged, praise him, but not until he has finished.

Should a puppy make a mess while the owner is not present, it is wrong to hit, shake or scold him as he will not understand what he is being punished for, only scold if he is *actually caught in the act*. (This also applies to destructive chewing.) To say, 'Oh, he knows he has done wrong by the look on his face' is fallacious; the puppy learns to recognise an angry expression on the owner's face, knows something unpleasant follows, and reacts accordingly. In this sort of situation he does not know what has elicited the owner's displeasure. Puppies kept indoors are usually confined to one room at night, often the kitchen or laundry room which has a washable surface, and in this case it is suggested that house training is assisted by putting newspapers down at night. Initially, it may be necessary to cover the whole floor or the area to which the puppy has access, but gradually, maybe only a few inches at a time, this can be reduced, and the papers remaining kept near to the door until only one or two spreads right by the door are required.

However, the time taken to train the dog to paper and to house train vary and are influenced by a variety of factors.
1. Location preference, i.e. where the puppy prefers to eliminate.
2. Surface preference, the puppy may like a particular surface.

3. Inappropriate punishment techniques of the owner – these may frighten the puppy who will try to escape from the owner.

4. Negative experiences outside the home when the puppy is frightened by noises, traffic or strangers, so he will eliminate only in the home.

5. Investigation of new areas – the puppy always sniffs around when first going out; this activity takes priority over elimination and, to overcome this, the best method is to confine this investigatory activity to one area until the puppy has satisfied his curiosity and eliminated. Then the walk can continue, thus acting as a reward to the puppy.

Rough, crude techniques of correction are quite out of place in paper and house training a young puppy.

Sometimes puppies indulge in what is known as submissive urination when frightened by the owner's gestures, shouts or smacks. The puppy may squat down or roll over and urinate. It is something which they grow out of, but any further threatening or punishment by the owner will exacerbate the problem. Ignore this occurrence and carry on as if nothing has happened by calling the puppy to you, praising warmly and giving a titbit. Absolutely nothing is gained by a harsh reaction on the part of the owner.

Crate Training

I now start puppies off in a crate, covering the floor with a piece of blanket or Vetbed, towel, etc. A puppy very quickly becomes accustomed to the crate and will readily go into it on command. This has many advantages for the owner: no chewing of unauthorised items, the puppy can be left in safety while the owner is out or asleep; and the crate affords protection for the puppy from boisterous dogs and small children. House training is also facilitated.

It is emphasised that confinement in the crate should not be for extended periods, and it should certainly not be regarded as an object of convenience or punishment.

Between 8 and 11 weeks the puppy should, if possible, be taken out of the crate during the night for reasons of elimination, and between 12 and 16 weeks he can stay in overnight, but he should always be taken outside as late as possible before the owner goes to bed. During the day it is to the advantage of both owner and puppy that there be as much contact as possible between them. After periods of activity, the puppy can be put in the crate to rest which is very important to large breeds like the Rottweiler.

Older dogs can also quite readily be trained to use crates, the crates I use for puppies are in fact adult size.

Always leave some toys in the crate for the puppy to play with, e.g. rubber ring, rubber bone, etc.

Crates are available in various sizes and are collapsible for easy carriage and storage.

Car Sickness

Certain breeds may be more susceptible to car sickness than others, and over the years many Rottweiler owners have had a problem accustoming their dogs to car travel. Not all of us are fortunate enough to have our puppy take to the car as the proverbial duck to water and this can be most upsetting for the puppy which feels – and usually looks – really queasy, and extremely irritating for the owner who has to clear up the mess and put up with the far from pleasant odour. In some instances, the mutual aggravation is sufficient for the owner to decide to leave the puppy at home, with the resultant loss of companionship and socialisation for the puppy.

While there is a school of thought which believes a dog just grows out of car sickness, it is much better for all concerned to take positive steps immediately the problem is identified to try to alleviate it. As far as car travel is concerned, the puppy or adult originally has no expectation of being sick when it gets into the car, but experience of car travel brings about such an association and some dogs begin to drool on getting into the car even before it starts to move. If you can prevent this association from forming, so much the better.

In the case of a new puppy, if possible take it in the car with another dog, a seasoned traveller, initially only for a couple of hundred yards or so up the road and back. Try to do this several times a day, gradually increasing the distance until the puppy can go on short trips to the shops, etc. At any signs of salivation or sickness, revert to a shorter distance or, depending on how quickly you want to accustom the puppy to car travel, use one of the proprietary products (for example Avomine) but check the dosage with your vet as young puppies should not have a full dose. Distance is slowly built up as is the puppy's confidence – and it soon realises that car trips are *fun!* The time taken to car train varies very much from individual to individual and in some cases considerable patience may be needed on the part of the owner.

For those owners who already have this problem, the strategy to adopt is to go back to the beginning. Put the dog in the stationary car with you, fuss it and then take it back into the house. Repeat several times a day until the dog is quite relaxed in these surroundings. Next, give the dog its food in the stationary car; again, repeat until it is happy. Then leave the dog alone in the car for a few minutes; repeat as before. Start the engine, stay with the dog, talk to it and fuss it, but do not drive off. Repeat until the dog shows no signs of stress; then and only then drive the car 25–50 yards down the road and back. It must be strongly emphasised that all this does not happen overnight and demands much patience and reassurance from the owner. Attempting to progress too quickly is a great mistake and can prolong the time necessary to overcome the problem. Increase the distance of trips very slowly and do not hesitate to revert to shorter ones if the dog becomes unhappy or unwell. When longer journeys are planned, it is a wise precaution to give suitable medication, always on an empty stomach and about one hour before setting out.

Unfortunately a large number of owners are simply not prepared to spend time in ensuring their puppy or adult is properly accustomed to the car; such a pity, as the well-trained companion dog enjoys this mode of travel and accompanying his owner on family expeditions, picnics or just to the shops. Furthermore, a sturdy Rottweiler in the back of the car gives a nice reassurance when travelling alone at night miles away from home.

Occasionally one finds a dog which becomes excited by passing traffic and leaps or scrabbles at the car windows when vehicles or people pass, often arriving at the destination a panting wreck with the owner often not much better. The solution, apart from not taking the dog any more, is to invest in one of the special car crates which prevent excessive movement, and also the two side windows can be darkened. Remember to ensure the dog is not in a draught from opened windows and that if uncrated, it does not stick its head out of the window. Dust and debris carried on the wind can cause damage to the eye.

Coming When Called
Being able to recall a puppy or adult should take top priority and it

is an exercise which many people find remarkably difficult to teach, largely, I suspect, because they did not start early enough and the puppy was allowed to be disobedient when young. Dogs need time to be dogs, free from human interference, so whatever you do, don't keep nagging the puppy so that when you do speak, he pays attention.

Teaching the recall cannot start too soon. Allow the puppy plenty of time to himself and when he comes to you of his own volition, bend down to his level and give lots of fuss and praise. Do not loom over him as this can be intimidating and do not grab him as he comes to you. You should represent a source of fun and pleasure as well as comfort, so have a titbit or a toy ready to give him to reinforce his idea of you. One day he will not come, but just jump around you, perhaps barking. At this stage do not make an issue of it, ignore him and walk in the opposite direction (it is assumed that all this takes place in home surroundings which are secure) and when he does come, praise as before. Grabs, angry shouts and smackings should never be used.

Proceed in this way and with all but the very strongest character the word 'Come' should eventually elicit an immediate response. With the more difficult puppy, have him on a lead or long line, and when you call 'Come', give a slight tug on the lead. When he comes give tremendous praise and reward. Build this up until he is reliable and then try him off lead, again in secure surroundings. When he reacts instantly try him in different locations (not near traffic or other distractions) until he is obedient in all situations. If he does not come immediately but wanders off and does his own thing before he condescends to obey, do not correct him when he comes by grabbing, shaking, smacking, etc. but go back to doing the exercise in a secure place. If he is persistently 'deaf', correction needs to be administered but he has to be cornered first and not checked when he comes to you. Give a good firm shake and a telling off, then back away and praise when he comes.

Rottweilers should be well under the control of their owners as some people may be frightened of being approached by large dogs off the lead and it is necessary to call them back from a distance, away from people, other animals or traffic.

In particularly intractable cases specialist advice may need to be sought, as there are other methods of teaching a dog to come when called which should be used only by an expert as split second timing is crucial.

In the early days of a puppy's life, it does so many things which are contrary to the owner's wishes that it seems to exist in a negative world of 'No, No, No'. Such an approach can have a depressing and alienating effect on the puppy. Instead, be positive. When he is doing something you do not want, distract his attention, call him to you, praise him, tell him to sit, and praise again. This is far better for his mental development than a series of negative commands and greatly assists in forging the bond between dog and owner.

Remember, too, when teaching a dog a new word, command or exercise that the time taken to learn this varies between individuals. However, on average, no fewer than twelve repetitions are necessary before the dog knows what is required. This means that the word or command is repeated on twelve different occasions, not just twelve times one after another! However, if it is something compatible with his desires, a dog will learn very much more quickly!

All important in training is the voice; variation in tone is an indispensable tool in conveying to the dog the owner's pleasure or displeasure. Here, perhaps, women handlers have the edge over men as they seem more able or willing to vary pitch – deeper and forbidding when the dog is erring, high and charged with excited pleasure when he is doing what is wanted. A dull, flat, continuous monologue is very boring and meaningless; there should be a marked contrast in tone between praise and blame, so the dog is well aware when he has pleased or offended.

Dogs enjoy playing with their own kind and with humans but, alas, some owners do not seem to know how to play. Rottweilers are very fun-loving and after a session of training, be it for manners or more advanced exercises like tracking or searching, a play session is very rewarding to the dog. A word of caution here, some men, and it is always men, seem to want to 'take on' a Rottweiler. They desire to overcome the power and arrogance of the male dog and tame it, such an end being accomplished by heavy wrestling bouts, huge jerks on the lead or 'stringing up' the dog. Even if the dog started off with a good stable temperament, it is unlikely to end up with one after this kind of treatment. Women handlers who have trained male Rottweilers to compete successfully in working trials/obedience/agility have managed to achieve excellent results without such strong arm tactics!

So, start as you intend to carry on with sympathetic but firm handling. Try to make any training session fun, and keep it short (about ten minutes for obedience exercises is quite enough). Don't nag, it produces boredom. Praise lavishly and don't strike or beat the dog – Rottweilers are not generally body sensitive but are very responsive to the voice. And do have a play session with your puppy or adult whether it is throwing a ball (large, solid rubber type), gloves, sticks or just a romp.

9   To Breed or Not to Breed

There is no doubt that many unsuitable dogs and bitches are used for breeding and it is an area where fallacies abound. For instance, the following commonly-held beliefs are not true:

1. It is necessary for the well-being of a bitch, regardless of quality, to have at least one litter.
2. The mating of any dog to any bitch results in 'lovely' puppies.
3. To mate any bitch to the latest or leading champion will result in a superlative litter.

These misunderstandings are not in the best interests of the breed, so let us look carefully at the situation.

The continued existence of animal species in the wild state depends on the survival of the fittest. Those less well adapted to cope with the problems and complexities posed by the external environment do not have long lives and are therefore less likely to pass on their genes to future generations. In the early days of domestication, it is logical that fitness for role was of paramount importance in the survival of dogs but, in modern times, the growing attention paid to external appearance and the increasing sophistication of veterinary medicine has meant that many puppies and dogs which were ailing in some way can be saved. What effect this has had on the general viability within breeds is open to question, with some exceptions such as the racing greyhound, packs of foxhounds, working varieties of gundog breeds, etc.

So what of the Rottweiler? As far as character is concerned, it is basically very representative throughout the breed. There are now many good looking and typical specimens, with a core of sound, healthy dogs. While in the early days of a breed it may be necessary to use mediocre animals for breeding due to lack of numbers and lines available, in breeds which have a large population much more choice exists, and only those animals which adhere closely to the breed standard in looks and character as well as being healthy and free from unsoundness, should be bred from.

Taking the fallacies mentioned above, no evidence exists that it is beneficial to the health of a bitch to have a litter. On the other hand, there is abundant proof that mating to the 'dog down the street' can produce disastrously untypical stock in looks and temperament as well as unsoundness. Further, the mating of a poor quality bitch to a well-known champion is unlikely to be satisfactory.

Before taking the decision to mate your Rottweiler bitch, there are several considerations which must be borne in mind: as mentioned above, the bitch should be typical of the breed in looks and character, and be sound. To the pet or novice owner, the assessment of quality for breeding purposes may be difficult, so it is suggested that the opinion of the breeder, if sufficiently experienced or if not, that of another experienced breeder or specialist judge of the breed, be sought.

Some of the factors which should eliminate a Rottweiler for breeding purposes are temperament problems (nervous or very aggressive) being assessed with due attention to the influences of the environment; soundness, whether there is a history of individual or familial problems, e.g. forehand lameness or hip dysplasia (in connection with the latter, the animal should be X-rayed and the hips scored through the official scheme); animals with, or animals having had, an operation for entropion; and adherence to breed type. This should be as laid down by the standard, with no exaggerations at either end of the height/length continuum. Serious constructional faults are marked lack of front (layback of shoulder) or hind (bend of stifle) angulation; back which is not straight and strong, i.e. sway (dipping) or roach (arched); incorrect occlusion of the teeth, i.e. overshot, undershot or wry (twisted bite) or with several missing teeth; front legs which are not straight, with weak pasterns, turning outwards in a pronounced fashion; dogs which are feminine in appearance and bitches which are masculine looking, however good their conformation.

Cosmetic considerations include eye colour – light yellow eyes are aesthetically objectionable; markings – care should be taken in using animals notably lacking in tan markings or with excessive markings. Long-coated dogs and bitches should never be bred from and should an otherwise good specimen have a short coat or be lacking in under-coat, or have too soft a coat, then the proposed breeding partner must be correct in these respects.

Having established that your Rottweiler bitch is typical of the breed, being physically and mentally sound, now give thought to the logistics of having a litter.

Space
Do you have the facilities for a litter: a room in the house which can be turned over to mother and pups, or an outside kennel, which can be heated as required, with an enclosed run? And most important,

bearing in mind that not all puppies go to their new homes by the age of eight weeks, is there enough space for those puppies which remain?

Conscientious breeders stand by their puppies, and should any need to be re-homed for any reasons (domestic problems, etc.) they take them back for assessment and re-homing with a suitable family. Are you able to do this?

'These are mine – keep your distance.'

Time

A litter of puppies is extremely time-consuming. After the initial halcyon period of two or three weeks, when the mother does the feeding and there is not much for the owner to do except feed the bitch and ensure the whelping box and surroundings are kept clean, comes the weaning, which means a great deal more involvement for the breeder. As the puppies grow, they become much more demanding, and any which do not go to their new homes by the age of eight weeks require individual attention and some socialisation to other humans and objects if they are to adjust properly to the outside world. Puppies which do not receive sufficient attention may find this adjustment to normal living conditions difficult or impossible. Much time must be spent on vetting the prospective purchasers, many of whom are very nice people but totally unsuited to owning a Rottweiler although they would probably be quite able to manage another less demanding breed.

Expense

Having a litter is expensive and can be very costly if things go wrong and the bitch and/or pups require veterinary attention. Starting with the bitch, she should be checked out by your vet before mating. She should be in good, peak condition, and be fed good quality food and supplements (as required), the amount increasing in the later stages of pregnancy. Also, there is the stud fee at the outset.

'Grub-up.'
A litter bred by Mrs
Feldmann.

Then with weaning, feeding costs really escalate as puppies need 4–5 meals a day and any deficiencies in diet are revealed very quickly by their poor appearance and growth rate. If all goes well, veterinary expenses are limited to maternal examinations before and after the litter is born, checking the puppies and tail docking and dewclaw removal, but if there are complications such as Caesarean section being necessary or the bitch having an infection which means the puppies have to be hand raised, costs rise rapidly, so one should budget for this. And, of course, there are the inoculations against parvo which are an essential part of any kennel routine.

Not least, there is the cost of advertising the litter since the likelihood of there being a queue of totally suitable, eager buyers is remote!

Whether or not to use a Rottweiler dog is a less complicated decision, there being no litter to rear and place in new homes. However, the same considerations apply as regards breed type, temperament and soundness which should be of the first order. Too frequently one encounters those who see their male dogs, quite regardless of quality, as a useful adjunct to the family income. What could be easier – a quick mating or two, money in the pocket and that's it! But it is not as simple as that. The knowledgeable and conscientious stud dog owner, whether a novice or experienced, will only accept bitches which are of a suitable age (minimum two years), good representatives of the breed, healthy and sound, and whose faults and virtues are complemented by the stud dog. The owner of the stud dog should take a positive interest in the resultant litter and actively assist in the placement of puppies if needed, a responsibility which is so often overlooked or even denied. The whole question of whether or not dogs and bitches are suitable for breeding is one which seems particularly difficult for pet or novice owners to comprehend. And in Rottweilers the fact that many pet-quality animals are used for breeding results in some ugly, untypical and unsound specimens being produced, so a major contribution which can be made to a breed by pet owner and breeder alike is to refrain from using sub-standard stock, otherwise the repercussions breed-wise can be extremely harmful and far-reaching. (This includes allowing well-known stud dogs to mate inferior bitches.)

Once you have established that your bitch is a good representative of the breed in every way, and is healthy and sound with a low hip score, choose the stud dog, and seek the owner's consent to its being used on your bitch well in advance.

Choice of dog must be made on the basis of his being strong in points where the bitch is weak and vice versa (no animal is, after all, perfect!) as well as on knowledge of the forebears of each, and on what system of breeding is to be adopted. Briefly, these are:

Outcross – dog and bitch not related (within four generations).

Inbreeding – breeding between related animals such as brother/ sister, mother/son, father/daughter, half-brother/half-sister.

Line-breeding – breeding between animals which are not closely related, e.g. grandfather/granddaughter.

Outcrossing

This is a commonly employed breeding strategy and the results when they come off can be good but variations of type within a litter should be expected. Outcrossing is almost exclusively used in Germany. It is often used by breeders with animals which are closely bred and new blood is deemed desirable. In this way the dominant characteristics are revealed and can then be consolidated by line or inbreeding.

Inbreeding

This is the quickest way to establish a line but it is fraught with peril for the unwary since harmful traits will surface as well as the desired ones and culling may well be required at birth and perhaps at adolescence. This method should ideally be used only by experienced breeders.

Line-breeding

With at least one common ancestor this is a safer method to fix the good points in a line. As with inbreeding, it is vital that the common ancestor(s) is/are of the highest quality as regards phenotype (actual appearance and character) and genotype (the genetic endowment to pass on these good characteristics). With Rottweilers not much really close breeding has been carried out in this country because established breeders seem to prefer line-breeding and prejudice against very close breeding is frequently encountered amongst the lay public.

Practicalities of Breeding

Before mating, worm your bitch and have her blood tested to determine her level of immunity to parvovirus and to ensure she is not anaemic. The time when a bitch ovulates, i.e. is ready for mating, is usually between the 11th and 14th day for Rottweiler bitches, but there are exceptions, with some being ready early (e.g. the 5th day) and others late (the 23rd day), so be prepared for this. A vaginal smear may be taken by your vet so that the progressive cell changes are seen and the optimum time for mating is clear. Such a technique is particularly useful when the mating partners live a long distance apart. Custom dictates that the bitch travels to the dog unless a special arrangement is made to the contrary. Some stud dog owners permit only one mating, others allow two, either on the following day or with a day in between.

If the journey is a long one, it is a kindness to allow the bitch ample time to have a rest and short exercise period before attempting a mating. Make sure before you take your bitch to the stud dog that you will be permitted to be with her all the time as with maiden bitches particularly the owner's presence acts as a reassurance. If the stud dog owner is unwilling to allow this, my advice is to go elsewhere.

If the dog has already sired a litter, the stud fee is payable at the time of mating, or, if he is unproved, the fee is usually paid when the litter is born. Sometimes a puppy (or puppies) are taken in lieu of stud fee and it is up to the owner of the bitch to decide whether to accept this option. Whatever arrangements are made, it is strongly urged that they should be in writing, with a copy to both parties, in order to avoid any possibility of misunderstanding. Contingencies which should be covered are, for example, what happens: (a) if there is only one puppy in the litter or (b) if the bitch's owner and the stud dog's owner both want to keep the same puppy?

To decide whether a bitch is in whelp or not may be difficult in big breeds like the Rottweiler, when the puppies may be carried high up or the litter is small. Palpation at four weeks by a vet is one method, but it is by no means infallible; or the bitch may be X-rayed (not a usual procedure). Most of us prefer to sit it out until the bitch well and truly reveals her secret.

For the first five and a half weeks she should be fed the same quantities of food and supplements as usual; thereafter the amounts should be increased. It is impossible to specify exact quantities of food as this must vary according to the needs of the individual and supplements such as SA37 and sterilised boneflour should be given according to the manufacturer's instructions. It is recommended that the food intake be split into three or even four smaller meals as it is easier for the bitch to digest smaller amounts at a time.

Although the normal gestation period is 63 days, some Rottweiler bitches decide to produce early (whelps are not normally viable if born more than one week early) while others hang on. Around the 56th day, have your vet examine your bitch as a routine precaution.

Prepare carefully for the litter. Items you need to have in stock are:
i Whelping box – these can be home-made and it is suggested you ask an experienced breeder about the design.
ii Vetbed, Dri-bed or similar covering to fit the whelping box (one piece on, one clean and one in the wash).
iii Loads of newspapers collected from friends or obtained from a newsagent as unsold/surplus. It is almost true to say you cannot have too many. They are for putting in the whelping box under the Vetbed and later in the kennel/run/floor.

iv Clean towels for drying the pups as they are born – *not* new ones as the lint comes off.

v A cardboard box with a covered hot-water bottle to put earlier pups in while another is born as they can run the risk of being squashed.

vi Cotton wool. Little blobs to wipe pups' noses and eyes and some squares taken off a big roll in case of having to help with breech pups (*i.e.* those born hindquarters first).

vii Pair of scissors with *rounded* ends (most important); for cutting umbilical cord if necessary.

viii Disinfectant such as Savlon.

ix A mug in which to place the scissors in the disinfectant solution.

x Small bottle of Friar's Balsam to put on the end of the cord of each puppy.

xi Small jar of Brands Beef or Chicken Essence – give a teaspoonful between whelpings – the bitch will appreciate it.

xii Large biscuit tin in which to put any stillborn pups for vet to check.

xiii Scales to weigh pups at birth.

xiv Pad and pencil to record times of birth, birth weight and whether placenta is delivered for each puppy. This last piece of information is very important as retained placentas can cause serious infection in the mother.

xv Some means of identifying puppies like scraps of different coloured wool.

Whether kept in a kennel or in the house, Rottweiler bitches in the main seem to like company when they whelp and owners are generally only too pleased to oblige. Indeed, I cannot think that a caring owner would not wish to ensure all was proceeding normally. Your vet should be informed when whelping starts so that he can give a contact number if any emergency arises.

During the week before whelping, the bitch may seem rather uncomfortable, uneasy and go off her food. She may need small meals often and it is quite usual for a colourless, sticky discharge to appear. Should this change colour to a yellowish hue or a dark green, check with your vet. Signs of whelping being fairly imminent are extreme unease and restlessness, heavy panting, scratching up of bed and usually a drop in temperature 24 hours before the puppies arrive. When any of these signs is observed, the bitch should be carefully watched as she could well decide to walk around scattering a pup as she goes for whelping can start very suddenly, with a 'one heave, one pup'!

The bitch should have been introduced to her whelping quarters a week before the puppies are due and, when whelping looks imminent, take her there and stay with her.

If a bitch strains for more than an hour without producing a puppy, contact your vet. It is a false economy to try to manage without veterinary assistance when problems arise as you may find yourself with a litter of orphan puppies to raise. Some bitches are very competent mothers, knowing what to do even with their first litter and there are no problems, whereas others just look at the mass which has just been produced and do nothing. Here the breeder must break the membranes which cover the puppies' heads and cut the cord. Allow a couple of inches, so that it is not cut too close to the body and tie with sterilised cotton above the cutting point.

If a puppy is presented in the breech position (hindquarters first) delivery may present a problem. Take a square of cotton wool, grasp the pup firmly and when the bitch pushes, try to draw the pup out. It is *vital* that the pup is not pulled straight out; it should be pulled in a circular downwards direction. Usually all that is required is slight assistance, but do not pull against the bitch's contractions.

Your vet should check mother and pups as soon as possible after the end of whelping to ensure that all is well with them (all pups viable, i.e. none with cleft palates or imperforate anuses) and that no placentas are retained. The bitch should be given an antibiotic injection.

After the litter is born, the bitch needs peace and quiet, so ensure that she is not disturbed by other animals, humans or loud noises. Occasionally a bitch may be so stressed by the nestful of demanding, wriggling little black bodies that she panics and cannot cope, so it is up to the owner to ensure that there is round-the-clock supervision and reassurance. This may demand considerable rearrangement of household routine, but it is a contingency which must be allowed for. Not many Rottweiler bitches are lacking in maternal skills, but new mothers can be clumsy, too, so it is best to remain on a 24-hour alert for the first few critical days and have a bed or sleeping bag in the whelping quarters.

Post-whelping diet should be fluid for 24 hours, followed by a resumption of 3 to 4 meals daily (1 or 2 meat and 2 milk). Lactation is a very demanding time for the bitch and places much stress on her, so generous feeding with good food is required to enable her to give the puppies the nourishment they need and to maintain her own condition.

It is very important that the environmental temperature of the 'nursery' should be kept constant; between 75–80°F in the case of bitches who are good mothers and stay with their puppies. With a less conscientious mother, an insulated heating pad for the whelping box should be obtained from your vet.

A condition which can occur a few days after whelping or towards the end of the lactation period is eclampsia. Large amounts of calcium are passed with the milk and if the bitch is given insufficient calcium and phosphorus (in the correct ratio) during pregnancy and lactation, eclampsia results. There may be stiffness or paralysis of the hindlegs, followed by convulsions if veterinary assistance is not sought. It is necessary for the bitch to receive an injection of calcium salts as quickly as possible. Complete recovery usually results.

Provided the pups are strong and sturdy, docking and dewclaw removal may be done at two days (certainly not later than four days). Some breeders perform this task themselves but, most emphatically, it is *not* something which should be attempted by novices. Controversy exists as to which method of tail removal is best: surgical amputation or rubber-banding, the method used with lambs. Both methods have their supporters. However, if you intend to have a vet carry out these procedures check well beforehand that he is willing to do so.

Opinions also differ on the time weaning should start. The overriding consideration should be the demands of the litter and the condition of the bitch. Leaving puppies on a bitch until they are 6 or 7 weeks old is not acceptable and at around $2\frac{1}{2}$–3 weeks many breeders start teaching the puppies to lap a proprietary puppy milk preparation, then creamed baby food, then finely scraped or minced beef, until the puppies are on 4–5 meals a day: 2 milk and 2–3 meat mixed with soaked puppy meal and supplements like SA37 and sterilised boneflour. It is best to give supplements once a day only.

While puppies should be nicely plump and firm to the touch, they should not be fat, ungainly and disinclined to move. Research now indicates that to feed for maximum growth contributes to skeletal disorders, since the puppy's developing bone structure is not strong enough to take the resultant stresses. Maybe big, heavy puppies – the Americans have a word for them, 'butterballs' – look far more impressive than smaller, wiry ones, but the latter are far more viable. Weight variation between litters is a fact of life and by no means always an indication of adult size, provided, of course, that the puppies are well reared from birth throughout the growing period. When the dam is inadequately fed during pregnancy and lactation and the puppies poorly nourished from weaning to the time they leave for their new homes, dietary deficiencies will affect development.

Trying to make money by 'doing a litter on the cheap', economising on food and heating as well as veterinary attention is mortgaging the health and well-being and even the lives of mother and pups. If a potential buyer is not satisfied either with the housing or condition of the family no purchase should be made. All puppies are appealing and though it may be quite hard to resist 'rescuing' one from an unsatisfactory environment, one's humane feelings may prove to be rather costly, in financial and emotional terms. The veterinary attention which may well be necessary, will be expensive, and it will be upsetting for you if the puppy is very sickly, unsound and suffering. Further, the purchase of such stock is actually reinforcing the bad breeder in his methods of rearing and dog keeping and encouraging him to persist in them. If he is left with stock on his hands for some time, he may well think again and hopefully decide that Rottweilers (and dogs generally) are not profitable enough for him.

Just as some bitches emerge from their maternal duties looking like well-fed, pampered ladies, others wear the stresses and strains all too visibly, showing weight loss, dull coat and lassitude. An excess of conscientiousness can result in the mother regurgitating her food for the litter after weaning and this activity deprives her of much-needed sustenance. To try to prevent this, do not permit the bitch to return to the litter for 1–2 hours after her meal (to leave it for longer than this is likely to distress her) and give more frequent, smaller meals. This regime should also be adopted for bitches which have lost condition as well as carefully regulated exercise.

A few weeks after whelping, the bitch usually has a mammoth moult and then grows a smart, shiny suit quite quickly. Novices sometimes worry about this coat shedding, but it is a normal sequel to having a litter. Grooming night and morning, if this is possible, speeds the departure of the dead hair.

Three youngsters from Mrs Blackmore's Gameyards Kennels. 'Ready to go.'

Placing Puppies in New Homes

The optimum time for this is 49 days (see Chapter 8) although it is not likely that all puppies will depart at this time, and it is essential that the ones which remain receive individual attention from the breeder.

But before all this happens, there is the task of screening interested enquirers. Indeed, before actually breeding a litter it is advisable to have some puppies booked and, if there are a lot of litters expected at one time, a large litter should not be kept since it is likely to prove difficult to find *suitable* buyers for all of the puppies. Unfortunately, the culling of a litter is often an emotional issue because the breeder (and/or the family) find it abhorrent to destroy life. Or puppies represent money and the thought of losing out is unpalatable in the extreme. However it seems infinitely preferable to rear only the number for which the right homes can be found.

Definitions of what constitutes a 'good' home vary enormously, depending on one's own attitudes, standards and values, and on how urgent the need is to home the litter (space, time and money have a bearing on this). The more puppies there are around, the quicker standards fall as there are too few of the right homes available. This is when problems arise!

Those people most likely to make a success of owning a Rottweiler are ideally those who have owned one before, to the satisfaction of dog and owner; people who have owned a guarding breed before (GSD, Dobermann, etc.); and those who will not leave the puppy alone all or most of the day. Married men who want a Rottweiler should remember that the puppy will be at home all day and the onus of feeding, house training and exercise will rest with those who are also at home. With a young family, the children's interaction with and attitude towards the puppy should be carefully monitored by the parents. A firm 'thumbs down' should be given to people who want a macho dog with which to show off; to those who want a ferocious guard; and to the partner who wants to give 'the other half' (or even the children) a 'little surprise present' for birthday, Christmas, etc.

New owners should have a house or flat with a properly fenced garden, secure against illegal access. Many young Rottweilers have been stolen from gardens and few of them are ever recovered. And anyone buying a Rottweiler should be prepared to take it to a training class.

No Rottweiler, whatever its age, should be sold 'over the telephone'. The potential owner should come to the breeder so that each may assess the suitability of the other. One should take endless time and trouble over the choice of a puppy which, after all, may be a companion for life. A very famous kennel in another breed springs to mind; no matter in what part of the country a potential purchaser lived, before they were permitted to have a puppy, apart from a personal meeting with the breeder, their home was always visited, if not by the breeder, then by a trusted friend who lived nearby. One cannot but admire such a caring and conscientious attitude. It may have lost them some sales but they had the satisfaction of knowing that everything possible had been done to ensure that the puppy went to a home with owners who would give the attention and affection needed. Perhaps not everyone can or will go to such lengths, although they can spend time talking to and assessing people interested in the breed, thereby disregarding to a certain extent the financial rewards of the sale of a litter and emphasising the consequences to the individual puppy's welfare. That is the very least a breeder can do.

Particular care must be taken when enquiries are received from abroad, because of the popularity boom Rottweilers are now suffering. Overseas dealers have sought to buy in whole litters or several puppies. Such enquiries should be consigned to the wastepaper basket. It is a great responsibility to send a dog out of the country; not only are the expenses incurred by the purchaser high, but also it is important for the development of the breed in the country concerned that imports are of a high standard. So often they are not. If you are prepared to sell stock overseas, do not let it be pet quality; that is most unfair. On the other hand, it is always a good idea to ask potential buyers to supply references from, say, their vet, another experienced person within the breed, a Kennel Club official, etc. Also enquire about the conditions under which the dog will be kept, who will look after it, etc. If no satisfactory reply is received, one may draw the obvious conclusions. In the United States, for example, several of the breed clubs have mandatory Codes of Ethics, and members are willing to help breeders as regards the suitability of the home offered. There are 'puppy mills' in production there, too, and, needless to say, their owners do not belong to Clubs which have Codes of Ethics.

Not surprisingly, new breeders are often flattered to receive enquiries from abroad, but it cannot be emphasised too strongly that the greatest care must be taken before sending a puppy to a country where the culture is very different from our own. For example, in the Far East attitudes towards dogs and dog keeping vary and their standards of practice fall far below what we would want for our puppies. Some breeders will not export to the Middle or Far East, especially Japan, for this reason. I make no apology for devoting so much space to the question of finding the right home for your Rottweiler. The breeder is the architect of the puppy's existence and, as such, should do everything possible to find it the best of homes. This takes time, money and integrity.

WORKING LINES

(shown opposite in corresponding positions)

Father	*Father*
WT Ch Bruin of Mallion	Rintelna The Bombardier
CD UDex TDex	CDex UDex
owner – Mrs Wait	owner – Mrs Macphail
The first Working Trials Champion	
Son	*Son*
WT Ch Lenlee Gladiator	Ch Horst from Blackforest
CDex UDex TDex PDex	CDex
owner – Mrs Osborne	owner – Mrs Macphail
	The first Champion to gain a Working
	Trials qualification.
Granddaughter	*Grandson*
Amelia of Torside and Blackforest	Blackforest Meister
CDex UDex	Maik CDex UDex
owner – Mrs Macphail	owner – Mrs Macphail

Just as the breeder received documents with his or her puppy, so should these be given to each puppy buyer: pedigree, KC registration certificate (if issued), diet sheet (sent beforehand), list of do's and don'ts, and dates of inoculations and wormings. Telephone the new owner a few days after the puppy has left to see if it has settled and urge the owner to telephone you should any problems or worries arise. And, of course, it should be a condition of sale that should the owner ever have to part with the dog at any time for any reason, then it should come back to you for re-homing. It is also helpful to both breeder and owner if it is made clear exactly what happens if the puppy develops any veterinary problem which could severely limit its function.

Sale of Dogs (and Puppies)

The Trade Descriptions Act (1968) is concerned with the sale of 'goods', and this applies to dogs. The general position is that all statements by the owner or breeder concerning dogs or puppies for sale must be accurate. It is an offence for false claims to be made, and ignorance is not a defence in law. Misrepresentation – for example giving a false pedigree or selling crossbred puppies as purebred – is an offence under civil law; so, too, is selling puppies as registered with the Kennel Club when they are not, the price for registered ones being higher than that for unregistered. In all three examples the breeder/seller would be liable for financial restitution to the purchaser.

Disagreement between purchaser and breeder often arises when the dog or puppy develops health problems such as parvovirus within a very few days of leaving the breeder, or becomes unsound with a defect such as hip dysplasia. It is advisable for this point to be clarified when the sale takes place, and a time limit agreed, beyond which the buyer could not claim against the breeder. One must be fair to both parties, and it is unreasonable for the buyer to expect recompense after the dog has been in his possession many months. See Appendix 4 for an example of a draft agreement between breeder and purchaser.

10 The Rottweiler as a Working Dog

The words 'working dog' embrace a whole variety of activities in which the Rottweiler can and does acquit himself with credit. The breed's role has changed over the centuries from cattle droving and guarding to cart-pulling and then to working as a police dog. It is this last role which ensured the Rottweiler's survival at a time (the turn of the century) when numbers had dwindled dangerously.

Kira (with actor Bryan Brown in a shot from *Parker*), the author's film/TV dog.

Police dog Dionis
Jager of the
Lancashire
Constabulary.

Nowadays, Rottweilers are used by the police, the armed forces, and the customs service as well as by private security organisations. In some countries, notably Scandinavia, they are used for mountain and forest rescue work. This is the 'official' side of the coin. But the breed's sphere of activities extends to other areas, too. A number of dogs have appeared in advertising, TV and films and in private ownership they take part in competitive events organised under the rules of the Kennel Clubs of individual countries and the FCI.

The worldwide supremacy of the German Shepherd Dog as the police and service dog par excellence makes it no easy task for other breeds to be accepted into the service working world in significant numbers. It was a momentous occasion for enthusiasts in England when a Rottweiler passed out from his training course, the first of the breed to become an operational police dog. This was in 1957 when Abelard of Mallion entered service with the Metropolitan Police of London. That force subsequently had three more at different times as did several other regional forces.

That the breed will be recruited extensively for police service is unlikely. There are several reasons for this: the universal image of the GSD's suitability for the role; the higher cost of the Rottweiler, both to buy and to rear; the fact that the Rottweiler takes longer to mature; and finally, perhaps, that the breed is less easy to train than the GSD, requiring a different approach and a handler able to appreciate this.

Those animals which have served as police dogs in this country have generally proved very good representatives of the breed, with their tracking ability and manwork of a high order.

The author's Blackforest Meister Maik, CDex UDex, an excellent tracker.

The armed forces do not use Rottweilers although there are rumours of one or two serving with the SAS, and the situation may change in the future. The breed is used by security organisations and it is believed that some unfortunately are exported overseas as guard dogs to hot countries where working conditions have excited adverse comments in the dog press. These working conditions seem totally unsuited for any dog particularly a breed which is susceptible to the heat.

As far as film work is concerned, the name of Mrs Joan Blackmore (formerly Woodgate), who has the Gamegards Rottweilers, is the best known. She has provided and trained dogs of various breeds as well as other animals for press advertisements, TV commercials and films and feature films. Her best known Rottweilers have been Panzer (Emil from Blackforest CDex), Condor (Gamegards Fire 'N' Rain), Sula (Gamegards Basula v. Sachenhertz) and Sieger (Rohirrim Sieglinde). Filming may sound glamorous but the reality can be somewhat different. Early rising to get on set in time, long periods of waiting with sometimes unrealistic and too exacting demands can make it rather fraught. When the finished product appears, some of the dog scenes, the pride of the owner/handler, may have vanished without a trace. But it's an interesting world.

Those who are interested in competing with their Rottweilers have three types of sport open to them: obedience, working trials and agility. All these are held under licence from the Kennel Club. Requirements for each event may be obtained from the KC and notice of dates and venues are given in the dog press, notably *Dog Training Weekly*.

Obedience

Obedience competitions are extremely popular, attracting large entries, and the standard of performance is extremely high. The exercises which have to be carried out are heelwork on and off lead, recall, retrieve, sit stay and down stay and in the more advanced classes a sendaway and scent discrimination where the dog must identify an article having its handler's or other person's scent and bring it back to the handler. While some Rottweilers take readily to competitive obedience and accept the high degree of precision required, others quickly become bored and their performance suffers.

If you want to train a Rottweiler for obedience, do not begin too early to instil precision in working. By all means have the dog retrieving, doing stay exercises and using its nose, but too much heelwork has a deadening effect. Many of the lagging Rottweilers we see may well have been trained too early and/or too intensively. Make sessions of heelwork with your dog short, at the double, or at any rate at a fast pace with lots of praise. Do not practise lots of sit during heel-work as this can slow the dog down. Teach sit as a separate exercise. To date, only one Rottweiler, Mrs Boyd's Champion Retsacnal Game-gards Gallant Attempt, has qualified to take part in Championship Test 'C' – no mean achievement. Others which have been well placed in open competition have been Mrs Hill's Sophie Sapphire and Mr Thompson's Nytecharm Satan.

Working Trials

Working trials offer Rottweilers more scope as much less emphasis is placed on precision and other exercises more stimulating to the breed are included, such as searching for articles, tracking, jumping, etc. All this takes place out of doors *whatever the weather*! To train a dog for trials requires dedication, time and equipment. It is a great handicap not to have one's own set of jumps. These can be made at home, given a modicum of skill, for although commercially available they are quite expensive.

Mr Nic Prebensen's Norwegian working trials dog Igax.

Training for trials begins when you bring your puppy home; you

socialise him to other dogs, animals, people and the urban world; he has toys to play with which he picks up and brings to you, all in play. He learns to walk on the lead without pulling and he is taught to stay in one place for very short periods of time. He searches for objects thrown into long grass, and as puppyhood advances, elementary tracking can be introduced. All this learning is carried out in a completely fun way without compulsion, so he has time to be a puppy. Formal-type heelwork is not introduced until he is around 9–10 months old and jumping is left until he is 18 months. Being a heavy breed, Rottweilers should not be allowed to put on excess weight and before starting to jump, a dog should be in a fit and not flabby condition, well muscled and on his toes. Jumping places a considerable strain on the forequarters of the dog when he lands, so it is strongly emphasised that immature and unfit dogs should never be jumped.

Many Rottweilers have done extremely well in trials and there have been three working trials champions, Mrs Wait's WT Ch Bruin of Mallion CD, UDex TDex, his son Mrs Buckle's (formerly Osborne) WT Ch Lenlee Gladiator CDex UDex TDex PDex and his grandson, Mr Hadley's WT Ch Jacinto's Bollero CDex UDex WDex TDex PDex. In addition, two show champions qualified in trials, my own Ch Horst from Blackforest CDex, the first champion to do so, and Mr Martin's Ch Princess Malka of Bhaluk, CDex UDex, the first champion bitch.

Agility

Agility competitions are the most recent additions to the working scene and are growing in popularity. Dogs are required to jump a variety of obstacles like an 'A' frame, hurdles, walls, water jumps, bush fences, triple bars, as well as negotiating a 'tunnel', a see-saw, a dog walk which is an elevated platform reached by planks set at an angle, and weaving poles. The dog which completes the course in the fastest time with the lowest number of faults is the winner. Few Rottweilers have so far entered open competitions and only one has been placed, Miss Liz Brendon's Breckley Soldier Boy CDex UDex, but it is a sport where the breed could do well as they are usually very accurate jumpers; whilst not being so fast as the ubiquitous Border Collie, they are very steady and not excitable which pays dividends on an exacting course. Though agility jumps are not so high as those in working trials, again I would emphasise that young, immature or unfit dogs should not be jumped.

Learning to negotiate the smaller jumps of the agility course gives a dog confidence and teaches it to be very nimble which helps when it has to face the more formidable trials jumps. But, apart from this,

Miss Ogilvy-Shepherd's Rhua taking part in an agility competition.

dogs of all breeds seem to enjoy agility, racing round the course with enthusiasm, and it certainly is a sport which has great spectator appeal.

In the early days of the breed, Rottweilers used to pull butchers' carts in Germany as part of their daily work. No formal competitions exist for cart-pulling but from time to time competitions are scheduled at agricultural or similar shows for the best decorated cart. Some of the turnouts are spectacular and Rottweilers have featured amongst the winners. Cart-pulling Rottweilers collect for charity at various events. However, it should be noted that in the United Kingdom it is illegal for a dog to pull a cart on a public highway, whether that cart is loaded or not. The aptitude for cart-pulling varies from dog to dog, some love it, while others loathe it. A careful introduction in various stages is necessary before harnessing the dog, first of all to get him used to the harness, then to the noise of the cart being pulled alongside by a human 'helper'. After that he can begin pulling a small plank of wood along the ground until finally he is harnessed to the cart. Initially, just let him stand still in order to become accustomed to the 'feel' of the shafts on either side of his body. It is advisable to have someone standing by during the last stage as just occasionally a dog may panic slightly until he is fully used to being constricted by the harness and shafts. Before making a public debut, don't forget to practise right and left turns, about turns, and having strangers come up and pat him – dogs drawing carts attract much attention.

Being a dog of high intelligence and a member of the working group, the Rottweiler is a breed which thrives on being given something to do. Lying around all day with nothing to stimulate him tends to make him lazy and unresponsive, so whether or not you have the time or desire to train for competitive events, train him to do something like carrying a shopping bag, taking a letter to the postbox with you, retrieving sticks, finding biscuits hidden in the house, etc. Let him use his brain in some way. He will enjoy it and the rapport between you will be increased. A trained and responsive dog gives so much pleasure and few of us can be immune to the admiration he elicits from the public!

For those of us who are able to train our dogs (and for trials especially, it is easier if you live in the country) apart from the fun of competing, we have the satisfaction of getting to know the individual dog intimately, to comprehend his strengths and weaknesses and to build up a mutually pleasurable relationship. In this way, one understands more about dogs in general, something which can be important these days when anyone owning a trained dog may be approached for advice by a stranger. A word of caution though. I have discussed the importance of taking your Rottweiler puppy to training classes and of exercising particular care in the choice of a class and instructor as by no means all are sympathetic to or experienced with the breed. Furthermore, there are some dogs which, at some stage of their development, react better to training outdoors on their own with an instructor or as a member of a small class.

Few Rottweilers, and none in this country, are trained as guide dogs for the blind as they are considered too large and most have a pronounced guarding instinct which is not wanted for dogs fulfilling this role.

Rottweilers are trained for mountain rescue work, notably in Scandinavia, where there is a vital role for a dog whose sense of smell can literally mean the difference between life and death to anyone so unfortunate as to be lost in the forest or buried by an avalanche. For this work the dogs have to be extremely fit, with no orthopaedic problems like hip dysplasia or osteochondrosis. Training starts quite early, with the dog being taught to find people in the forest just a short distance away from the path. Tremendous praise is given as well as a food reward in the initial stages of training. The rescue dog wears a special collar with a leather mouthpiece hanging down on to the dog's chest. When a missing person is found, the dog is taught to 'flip' this into his mouth and return to his handler, so signifying he has discovered someone. He then takes the handler back to the spot where he made the discovery of the missing person.

The same principles are used for training dogs to find missing persons in snow conditions except that during training the helper is actually buried in the snow! There are insufficient police or military dogs available to find people who are lost in snow or forest, so civilian owners train their dogs for rescue work and are called upon to help when people go missing. Distances are great, and it is essential to be able to set a dog searching as soon as possible because of the weather conditions and the risk of dying from exposure. An extensive network of trained dogs and handlers has become very necessary.

Knaussen's Dino carrying a pack on a cross-country expedition in the Norwegian mountains.

With three other Rottweiler owners, I attended a week's training course run by the Norwegian Rottweiler Club for beginners and more advanced dogs and owners. It was a most interesting and worthwhile experience; a copybook example of how to train by totally inducive methods. To search for hours on end in difficult terrain, without flagging, a dog must *want* to do it and no amount of compulsion or harsh treatment can make him.

The Rottweiler is nothing if not versatile, fulfilling a variety of roles very successfully. Some are used by their farmer owners to work cattle; a very few work sheep; and one hears of the occasional dog which goes out with the guns to retrieve game like Mrs Trowbridge's Erland Ramses UDex, whose autumn and winter Saturdays are spent picking up dead and wounded birds, a task at which he is very skilful, having an extremely 'soft' mouth and keen nose.

Only fairly recently has it been realised that dogs can be used in a therapeutic way to help the sick and lonely. In 1982 the charity PRO-Dogs launched the PAT-dog scheme (PRO-Dogs Active Therapy Dog) whereby dogs, pure or cross bred, with friendly and outgoing temperaments are taken by their owners to elderly persons' homes, long-stay wards in hospitals, childrens' homes and psychiatric wards. Simply sitting and stroking a responsive animal helps people relax and come out of themselves. Several Rottweilers have joined the ranks of PAT-dogs – Mrs Trowbridge's Erland Ramses UDex, my own Auslese Nemone from Blackforest and her daughter Blackforest Madame Pero, Mrs Houlihan's Frederick of Alfreton and Mr Evans' Mwyfanwy Sizuki.

The average owner wants his dog to be a good guard, to deter potential wrongdoers and to give a feeling of security to the family. However, a novice's understanding of what the dog will do is often uninformed, to say the least, and it is not uncommon for a puppy of three months to be expected to be a resolute guard! The guarding instinct is one which develops as the dog matures. While there is a genetic endowment, it is only by socialisation, which gives the dog confidence to meet all sorts of situations, that its full potential is realised. There is no set age when a youngster first starts to guard; it varies considerably and owners should be aware of this, not becoming impatient with the dog and on no account trying to 'hot it up' – a very great mistake. Rottweilers are excellent natural guards and should be allowed to develop at their own pace.

11 The Show Scene

An activity involving dogs which gives great pleasure to devotees is entering conformation classes at shows licensed by the Kennel Club and held every week throughout the country. Sometimes puppies, or adults, are purchased specifically with this purpose in mind, whilst other owners just drift into it, a friend often suggesting that they should 'have a go'.

Mrs Thelma Gray's Rozavel Arnolf v.d. Eicher Ruine, the first male Rottweiler to be imported into Britain in 1936, off to the Show.

Evaluation of Rottweiler puppies as potential show specimens is by a combination of eye, experience and luck, for no one can say with absolute certainty that a particular puppy is going to hit the highspots. So while 'fliers' do occasionally come from unexpected sources, they may be one-offs and it is best to go to a line which has a record of show successes. While the choice of a show puppy is almost exclusively based on its conformation and balance, the question of temperament should not be overlooked. The outgoing, lively, personality-plus puppy whose very attitude says, 'Here I am, look at me' has a distinct advantage in the show ring.

I am often asked what physical qualities to look for in a puppy to justify the investment of time, money and hope. At seven to eight weeks, one sees a little miniature adult. Some faults which are then visible do not usually right themselves, e.g. undershot mouth, a sway or dippy back, eyes which are markedly light, noticeably large ears, fine muzzle, straight shoulders and stifles, front legs which turn outwards at the pasterns, and back (couplings) too long. After that age puppies may grow every whichway and assessment is difficult or impossible. The impatient owner just has to switch off for a few months.

At six to nine months the picture becomes somewhat clearer with the head taking shape, the overall proportions – height to length of body and the reach of neck – likely to be permanent as will be eye colour, size of ears, bone and pigmentation (or lack of it) of inner lips and gums. Excessive skin on the head, round the throat and neck will probably remain. All the permanent teeth should have erupted; any missing ones will not now come through, even though they may actually be present in the gum. There should be a good scissor bite, i.e. the top teeth (incisors) come down over those in the lower jaw. Any teeth which are barely scissor or pincer may go undershot within the next few months. Movement, too, should have begun to tighten up, given that the puppy has been exercised as befits his age. Faulty movement due to faults of construction like straight shoulders or stifles, weak pasterns, tied elbows, etc. will remain. Given good overall conformation, movement should tighten up with maturity as should the muscling-up which comes with maturity and suitable exercise.

Features which are still developing at this stage are the breadth and depth of the body, brisket, spring of rib and the loins, which may well show some tuck-up now, and sometimes the croup which may be too sloping or too upright. The topline may be rather 'soft' when moving – it does not remain firm – even though it may be straight in stance. So the assessment of a puppy's or young dog's ultimate show potential is an ongoing exercise. Dogs develop at different rates, and while it is possible to eliminate for some faults fairly early on, patience is needed to see what the finished article will look like. And patience is not an easy thing to preach. Too many want an 'instant' Rottweiler, an 'instant' winner.

Before being taken to a show, it goes without saying that any animal of whatever age should be in top physical condition, groomed to perfection with clean teeth and short nails. He should also have been well socialised to the outside world and received some ring training. Without prior exposure to show-type conditions, where a stranger will examine him and there will be other excited dogs, he will be at a distinct disadvantage.

For this purpose ringcraft classes are run by show societies and training clubs (lists are held by the Kennel Club). There are also privately organised clubs, and vets or other Rottweiler owners can often recommend a suitable one. Ringcraft classes on their own are

Mr L. Price's Ch. Jagen Blue Dale. This is how showing should be done.

not enough, and the young hopeful should be introduced to as many sights, sounds and noises as possible as well as becoming a seasoned car traveller. Shows can be quite noisy affairs, especially if they are held outdoors in conjunction with, say, an agricultural event, and dogs which are poor travellers or insufficiently socialised will not look their best.

Like other large breeds, Rottweilers are slow to mature and may not reach their best until the age of two or more. Certain individual specimens and lines mature quickly and resemble small adults even as early as six months, but those that develop in this way are likely to reach their peak too soon and coarsen with age, thus not fulfilling their promise. It seems preferable to have a dog which matures slowly and even goes through a 'gangling' stage; these dogs seem to be the ones that last.

It is best to start off your puppy at small shows or matches run by canine societies and progress to the larger shows as both you and your dog gain experience. Should there be no ringcraft class sufficiently near for you to attend, visit some shows yourself to see what goes on and ask the breeder of your dog for some helpful hints.

Buy the correct equipment: a check-type collar of leather or metal (not nylon for a large dog) and a leather lead. At a show where the dogs are benched, you will need an ordinary non-slip leather collar and a benching chain to attach it to the bench. Not infrequently, Rottweilers have been chained up when wearing a check-type collar. This is highly dangerous. If he slips or gets off the bench, he can choke or, at best, receive a nasty fright. So make sure you use the correct type and that the benching chain is not kept too long.

Showing dogs can be enjoyable and provide an absorbing interest but there are several points to remember. First and foremost, consider the welfare of your Rottweiler. At a benched show take a rug, strip of carpet or at least several thicknesses of newspaper to put on the bench for the wooden surface can be rough. Take a bowl for fresh water, always available on site, but do not feed just before, during or just after a show. Do not leave your dog on the bench unsupervised for hours on end while you are socialising at the bar or ringside; go back to him frequently to see he is all right and take him off the bench for exercise several times during the day. Should he be restless or noisy on the bench or aggressive to dogs or passers-by, then it is your duty to remain with him. An aggressive or noisy dog can absolutely ruin the day for those benched nearby and it can put novice or young dogs off shows for life. You have a responsibility to keep your Rottweiler under control at all times – in the ring, outside the ring and on the bench. Treat other owners and their dogs as you would wish to be treated yourself.

Father. Mrs
Elsden's Ch.
Chesara Dark
Charles.

Son. Mrs Slade's
Ch. Caprido
Minstrel of
Potterspride.

Grandson. Mrs
Butler's Upend
Gallant Theodoric.

Showing dogs is a sport and should be regarded as such. If a particular judge's opinion is not to your liking, you do not have to enter under that person again. To win or lose gracefully is a habit which every exhibitor should cultivate. It makes the day more pleasurable for all concerned and the dog is still the same one you set out with that morning! To show your dissatisfaction at the judge's placing by tearing up your award card or being rude to the judge merits a report being made to the Kennel Club about your conduct. To make unpleasant remarks at the ringside about other dogs, exhibitors or the judge is the height of bad manners and shows a total lack of good sportsmanship. The show world can do without those people.

12   Rottweilers Around the World

Many countries, apart from Germany, have large Rottweiler populations and the breed has shown a steady rise in popularity. While a Rottweiler is a Rottweiler anywhere in the world, demands and preferences may vary from country to country.

Austria

Austria is unique in that one branch of its armed forces, the Army, uses Rottweilers almost exclusively in its dog section. There are about 250 dogs bred by the Army at the Dog School just outside Vienna.

A class of recruits at the Austrian Army Dog School.

The civilian head of the School, Herr Adolf Ringer, is in overall charge of the training of dogs and handlers, selection of suitable dogs, choice of breeding partners and rearing of puppies. All the dog handlers are civilians and the selection process operates at two levels: personal and familial. As all army dogs live as part of the family, it is critical to the success of the man-dog team that the home environment is suitable. In this country the current view is that a service dog, civilian or military, operates at maximum efficiency when kennelled outside, all other variables being equal. The Austrian Army Dog School considers that advantages are conferred on the animal by human contact of all types in all circumstances. Also that it is important that the dog is under the effective control of the handler at all times so that there are no negative influences at work. However a kennel is provided for occasions when the handler has to be away from home.

The dogs and bitches used for breeding are all fully trained military dogs and no Rottweiler which fails to achieve working status is used for breeding. The bitches come to the School for whelping two weeks before the due date, remaining there for five weeks after the puppies are born, after which they return to their handlers. All pups in a litter are raised – a Federal law makes it illegal to put down puppies unless they are diseased. Retired Army dogs are not destroyed, they live out their time naturally.

Civilian-owned bitches may be mated to military dogs, but before a bitch is accepted, she is given a thorough character assessment. If she fails, then a mating will not be permitted. Potential recruits to the working dog force receive a radiographic examination of hips, shoulders, elbows and pasterns at the age of six months and ten months, and at six months and 12–15 months working potential and character qualities are tested. These two types of examination eliminate about one-third of the dogs. Those which are rejected are given to families as pets without papers. At the six months' test, borderline cases may be retained and then reassessed at the second test. Basic training lasts three months and is completely inducive. Spiked collars are never used and there is much emphasis on praise and encouragement, with no rough handling. When trained and on station, dog and handler are visited by the Chief Trainer and a vet twice a year. Both dog and handler are re-tested with the results of each six-monthly test being fed into the computer. When I visited the kennels there were about sixty dogs (mainly on courses) and the overwhelming impression was of their activity. They were not large Rottweilers as it is felt that the medium-sized dog is the most viable working proposition, and all were fit and hard and extremely workmanlike in conformation.

Australia

Because of its very stringent quarantine arrangements, Australian Rottweilers are based almost entirely on British imports; even though the UK is recognised as a rabies-free area, English dogs still have to undergo a period of quarantine upon arrival in Australia.

The first import from England died during the sea voyage and it was not until 1962 when Captain Roy-Smith emigrated from England with his family and two dogs, Rintelna The Dragoon (Droll v.d. Brötzinger Gasse SchH2 - Vera v. Filstalstrand) and Rintelna The Chatelaine (Ajax v. Fuhrenkamp - Rintelna Lotte v. Oesterberg) that the first of the breed entered the country. Pilgrimsway Loki (Rintelna The Bombardier CDex UDex - Brunnhilde of Mallion) was sent out to Mr Mummery in 1963 and he then imported a bitch Lenlee Gail (WT Ch. Bruin of Mallion - Lenlee Neeruam Brigitte CDex UDex). Next, Colonel Pettengell brought in Chesara Dark Impression in 1967; she was to be a great influence on the breed. 1972 heralded a whole host of imports from England, mainly into Victoria and New South Wales. In 1978, the first Rottweiler from Germany arrived, Catja v.d. Flugschneise. At that time, in order to qualify for entry into Australia, it was necessary for any dog other than from the United Kingdom, Eire and New Zealand, to undergo six months' quarantine in the UK, followed by a further six months' residence, before being allowed entry, and then there was still a period of three months' quarantine in Australia, a goodly slice out of a dog's life, as well as having to suffer at least three changes of home. So it was a venture not to be undertaken lightly. Fortunately, the four animals so far brought in from outside the UK and New Zealand have been of much value to the breed: Catja (and four puppies from her litter, born in England, by Ch. Castor of Intisari), Felix v. Magdeberg and Echo v. Magdeberg, both imported by Colonel Pettengell ('Auslese'), and the US dog, Powderhorn Fetz of Wencrest owned by Mrs Pat Hall ('Stromhall').

Since these four dogs were imported, the regulations for importing stock have been relaxed to the extent of permitting dogs from outside the UK, Eire and New Zealand to have to remain for only one month's residential period in the UK instead of the previous six months, followed by two months' quarantine in Australia.

In the early days, much close breeding took place because of the limited number of dogs and bloodlines, but the widening of the gene pool brought about by the recent importations must be very encouraging to serious breeders.

English breeders/judges who have visited Australia have been impressed by the enthusiasm and dedication they have found and the quality of the best stock.

Apart from shows, where champions are made up on a points basis, much emphasis is placed on the working side of the breed and a number of dogs hold obedience and tracking qualifications as well as achieving high honours in the show ring. Notable in this respect was Mrs Hall's Stromhall Torrey CD CDex UP TD who had a brilliant show career, was a notable working dog and the sire of many typical sound puppies. It was his owner's ambition to make him a dual champion (show and working), the first in Australia, but this hope was not to be realised as he was tragically shot at the age of six.

Mrs Hall's Australian Ch. Stromhall Torrey.

The lines of the long-established breeders Colonel Pettengell ('Auslese') and Mr Mummery ('Heatherglen') lie behind many of today's kennels, and the recent importations from Germany made by the colonel, their pedigrees containing some illustrious names, will be of the greatest benefit to the breed.

Several breed clubs exist but with the vast distances involved activities must be organised on a regional basis and a variety of events such as demonstrations, cart-pulling, agility, etc. take place. The Rottweiler can now be classified as a popular breed and as registrations show it is one of the fastest growing.

The Caribbean

A great deal of interest in the Rottweiler, particularly as a guard, has

Colonel and Mrs
Pettengell's Auslese
Bold Royston in
harness.

been shown in Jamaica, Barbados and Trinidad and Tobago. Initially, the breed made a slow start but as it became better known, more and more people were attracted to its sterling character and redoubtable guarding instincts.

Trinidad
The first import, Bhaluk Princess Barbella (Ch. Ero v. Buchaneck –

Elsa from Blackforest) was brought in by Mrs Margaret Wattley. She achieved her championship and qualified CD, as well as producing three litters, two by artificial insemination by the Venezuelan dog, Landsrecht von Canaina. During the period 1968–1980 several more dogs were imported, mainly from England, but not all fulfilled the hopes of their importers. Interest in the breed grew apace, and from 1981 onwards many more dogs came into the country, mainly from the United Kingdom, but also from neighbouring Caribbean islands, one from Germany and two from the USA.

So far there is no specialist club for Rottweilers although numerically stronger breeds like GDSs, Dobermanns and Boxers have them. Several shows are run each year with well-known international judges. Obedience classes are also run which are very necessary for owners new to Rottweilers.

A few years ago some dogs were in service with the police but at the moment only GDSs are used. So the work Rottweilers do is to guard the home and family and also factories and shops where they are loose at night. Because of the extremely high cost of importing dogs, they are generally valued and well cared for.

Holland

The Rottweiler is a popular dog in Holland and there are about 6,500 dogs there. Records indicate that the first Rottweiler to be exhibited at a show was named John; this was in 1910, but no further details about him are available.

In 1912 nine Rottweilers were being exhibited, and the number increased very slowly until the outbreak of World War II. After the war there was some prejudice against German breeds so there was no significant growth in numbers. Around 1960 there were about 600 dogs in the country and numbers steadily grew. Registrations of puppies were: 1975–645; 1980–890; 1984–1,887.

Dogs which have proved important in Dutch breeding are: 1972–1976 – Nino v.d. Brantsberg; 1975–1980 – Harras v.h. Brabantpark and Int. Ch. Benno v. Allgauer Tor; 1980–1983 – Simba v.h. Brabantpark and Fulco v. Tannenwald; 1983 – Int. Ch. Duuck v.d. Nedermolen. The Dutch Rottweiler Club has been most concerned with hip dysplasia, and under the guiding hand of the late Dr van de Velden, research into the disease was undertaken at the University of Utrecht, where a breeding programme using Rottweilers was initiated. There are strict regulations for breeding for members of the Dutch Rottweiler Club which include:

1. Dogs without official pedigrees issued by the Dutch Kennel Club must not be bred from.
2. All dogs and bitches must be X-rayed for hip dysplasia and be

declared to have normal or near-normal hips.

3. Animals which deviate significantly from the standard must not be bred from.

4. Nor those which have been found by the governing body of the Dutch Rottweiler Club to transmit serious faults and/or deviations when used with bitches of varying bloodlines. (These recommendations are published in the Club magazine.)

5. All animals must have passed the Dutch Rottweiler Club's character test or have obtained a Dutch police-dog certificate (KNPV).

6. All animals must have been graded at least Very Good by two different judges at official shows.

7. Bitches must not be bred from more than once a year, nor under the age of 24 months.

Mr G. Kuyper's Int. Ch. Duuck v.d. Nedermolen.

8. Dogs must not be used for breeding under the age of 24 months.

Generally, dogs which have been excluded from breeding in foreign countries cannot be used, but there are certain exceptions. Exceptions can also be made from the regulations as a whole. However, there have been only two exceptions and such dispensations, with reasons for them, must be published in the Club newsletter.

Breeders must inform the Club in writing that a mating has taken place, and of the birth of a litter, including the number of dead pups, within fourteen days of the event taking place. If the governing body of the Club considers it necessary, they or an expert on their behalf must be allowed to inspect the litter. The breeding regulations are very strict. The Club will assist with the sale of puppies from litters which meet the requirements of the breeding regulations and also, if wanted, with the choice of breeding partners for suitable animals.

There are no Rottweilers in service with the police or army nowadays.

Israel

Israel has a small population of Rottweilers, about 300, with no large breeding kennel. Most dogs are with pet owners who value them as guards, and few people keep more than two or three.

Captain Dov Rosental's Israeli Ch. Banko Doodaéem.

The first dogs came in from Finland in 1968, and in 1975 six dogs were imported from Germany for guard duties with the services. A few others were brought in from other countries, but as yet type has not been stabilised.

The civilian police use mainly German Shepherds today but there are some Rottweilers with the Army which are used for guarding, attack work and special duties.

The Israel Rottweiler Club was formed in 1976 and contains a band of very dedicated enthusiasts.

Dr Carla Lensi's Pegghi della Riva Petrosa.

Italy

Most historical sources agree that Rottweilers originated from a Roman breed which was crossed with local dogs, but it was not until 1939, according to the records of the Italian Kennel Club, that the Rottweiler returned to Italy, perhaps due to the German military authorities. In that year eight were registered, six in 1941 and then none until 1952. During the 1950s a significant kennel, 'Rotargus', was formed by Dr Sala and Dr Colombo of Como who imported some notable dogs from Germany. Both men had been prisoners of war in a German camp and had been greatly impressed by the character of the Rottweilers which had been used as guard dogs at the camp, so after the war they started a breeding kennel. Some of the dogs they imported were Ero vom Hackerbrücker, Rita vom Köhlwald, Ero vom Butzensee and Alice vom Forchenkopf, and in the Progeny Class at the 1960 Milan Show the 'Rotargus' group consisted of 20. The 'Rotargus' kennel ceased breeding during the early 1960s and an attempt by Mr Bruno Piccinelli in the late 1960s to revive interest in the breed failed.

In 1972 Dr Carla Lensi and her husband, subsequently granted the kennel name 'della Riva Petrosa', imported the litter mates Nick and Nelly v. Kallenberg and in 1973 Diana v.d. Hofreite who became an Italian Brood Bitch Champion. Her son, Italian Champion Ives della Riva Petrosa (by Fetz v.d. Waldachquelle) has proved to be an excellent stud force.

Another German dog, Carlo v. Liebersbacher Hof, was imported by Ms Tosi. Mated to Diana, he produced several good offspring including Jessica della Riva Petrosa which achieved top honours at the World Championship Show at Verona in 1980. Jessica with Dingo v. Schwaiger Wappen produced another excellent stud force in Asso della Riva Petrosa. Two other kennels which appeared on the scene in the 1970s and early 1980s, owned by Mrs Alda Rossini and Mr Giribaldi respectively, are no longer active and made no significant contribution to Italian breeding. Registrations have slowly increased as follows:

1974–28; 1975–61; 1976–72; 1977–71; 1978–150; 1979–109; 1980–180; 1981–195; 1982–187; 1983–135; 1984–231.

Today there are about 600–700 Rottweilers in Italy.

A specialist club for the breed was formed in 1979. It does not issue pedigrees and there are no regulations for breeding whatsoever.

Rottweilers are not used by the police, customs or army. However, as a working breed, the title of Italian Champion is only awarded if, in addition to show wins, the dog has passed its certificate working test (CAL). There are three sections to this: indifference to people; indifference to gunshots; and attack work on a criminal wearing a sleeve. The mandatory requirements for show wins are: two CACIBs (equivalent to our challenge certificate) obtained at international shows; two CACs (as above) obtained at national shows; a grading of Excellent and first place at a special show.

Malaysia

Rottweilers enjoyed a degree of popularity in the late 1970s but the interest was short-lived. However, since 1982, the breed has found public favour again and registrations in 1983 were 86 while in 1984 they were 235.

Imports are mostly from Australia, New Zealand and the UK, and mostly by dealers.

So far, only one Rottweiler has achieved a Best in Show award at a Malaysian All-Breeds Championship Show: the bitch Kuhnheit Frau Giselle, imported by Mr K. K. Yeo from Australia.

New Zealand

The first Rottweiler was imported into New Zealand from Australia in 1970: Auslese Montrachet was bred by Colonel Pettengell, and the first litter was whelped in 1975, out of a bitch which came into the country from England en route to Australia. Attila Bathsheba was mated to Upend Gallant Alf before leaving England and all the litter except one went on to Australia.

The first recorded NZ Champion was Ch. Asgardweiler Winston (owner K. Murphy) of 'Auslese' breeding, imported from Australia. In 1974/5 there were only two Rottweilers registered in New Zealand and the breed was ranked 88th, but in 1983/4 there were 388 Rottweilers registered (52 litters) and the ranking was now 8th! There were around 107 active breeders.

A breed club was formed in 1978. The Rottweiler Club is based in Auckland, at the top of North Island, and it held its first championship show in 1984. Due to the meteoric rise in popularity, a second club was formed in 1983 when the Central Rottweiler Club was born out of a need to give the breed some foundation in the middle area of the country (based in Wellington). It has a demonstration team and intends to foster the working image of the breed; the first Open Show was held in 1985. Conditions of entry for dogs are the same as those in force in Australia and imports have come in mainly from that country with about eight from the UK.

Republic of South Africa

Records show that between 1939 and 1945 only one dog was registered each year, while from 1945 to 1956 none was registered. Then registrations slowly started to increase as follows: 1956–57–20 dogs, 1965–70–10, 1970–71–27, 1972–73–50 dogs. In 1973 the Rottweiler Working and Breeding Association of Transvaal was formed by Dudley Bennett ('Tankerville') and from about that time, the Rottweiler started its climb from obscurity, with soaring registrations: 1975–76–679 dogs to 1983–84–3,975, and it is now the second most popular breed on the Kennel Union of South Africa breed registration list, with GSDs being just ahead.

Most dogs are owned by members of the four million white population and the majority (80%) live in and around the Transvaal. This dramatic rise in numbers is attributed to the riots which occurred in the 1970s and the many burglaries which are a common feature of today's living, so people want powerful guard dogs. The GSD is still the most widely used breed; Rottweilers are second and Bull Terriers third, Dobermanns have fallen from third place and are still declining rapidly.

Dudley and Pamela Bennet's South African Ch. Tankerville Digby.

Although the primary interest was as a guard dog, Rottweilers started to appear at shows and one dog, Ch. St Tuttston Bastian of Tankerville, the foundation stud dog of the Tankerville kennels, was widely shown throughout the country, bringing the breed to the notice of many people who had never seen it before. Winning over sixty best of breeds, appearing on the front cover of a popular weekly magazine and being a 'one dog' demonstration team for the Club, made him a most valuable ambassador for the breed. One of his progeny, which included many champions, was Tankerville Heidi, Rottweiler Bitch of the Year from 1979–83 inclusive. Mated to the English import, Ch. Upend Gallant Luke of Tankerville, two of the resultant progeny, Ch. Tankerville Digby and Ch. T. Debbie have been given top honours by noted Rottweiler specialist judges from overseas in record show entries. This is greatly to the credit of show 'buffs' because the distances which they have to travel are great.

Dogs have been imported from Germany, Holland, England, Austria and Denmark, and their contribution to the breed has varied. At present, the breeding system in South Africa is similar to that in the UK – there is no official control. Unfortunately, many good dogs are lost to breeding because they are kept as pets, live in rural areas and are not brought to shows where their worth could be seen. Other Rottweiler clubs have been or are in the process of being formed and the breed has a loyal following of devotees, with many events being arranged. The RWBA recently introduced aptitude tests for Rottweilers, modelled on the Danish test.

Scandinavia – Norway

The Rottweiler is an old breed in Norway, and although the first one, a bitch named Florry, was registered in 1919 there were specimens of the breed in the country as far back as 1910. Founded in 1933, the Norwegian Rottweiler Club is directly responsible to the Norwegian Kennel Club, and today has about 600 members, with about 400 registrations. Almost all breeders follow the recommendation to use only stock free from hip dysplasia for breeding which has been in force since 1960. Today the percentage of animals with this defect is approximately 28%. During the last few years, breeders have become concerned with the problem of osteochondrosis in the elbow joint, and routine X-raying to gain more knowledge of the problem began seven years ago.

Most Rottweilers in Norway are companion and family dogs, but their working and obedience qualities are well known, many of the breed having obtained the title Norwegian Obedience-Champion.

During the 1950s the breed was dominated by imports, but in the 1960s the well-known Champion Ponto appeared on the scene. Bred in Sweden in the Fandangos kennel, his most famous litter contained Fandangos Fairboy (later to become an International Champion) who had a very great influence on the breed throughout the whole of Scandinavia. His name appears in many pedigrees of English Rottweilers through his son, Champion Chesara Akilles. Another influential dog was Norwegian Champion Kim, not only an exceptionally good show dog but also a winner of many obedience trials. One of his sons, Dick, who became a police dog, was also a very good show dog but did not achieve his show title. Dick was mated to a Swedish import named Stäppens Bärbel and the resulting litter contained three lovely dogs who all became champions: Solbro's Kim, S. Sitra and S. Chaka. Champion S. Sita also became an obedience champion. Unfortunately, this line was not taken care of and now has few descendants.

The early 1970s saw a greater recognition of the Rottweiler as a working and police dog and during this decade there came the first woman handler of a mountain rescue dog, a Rottweiler named Hard-Jehka.

Many dogs are trained for mountain rescue work in the snow, and in forest rescue. Such is the density and extent of the forests that it is all too easy for children and even adults to stray off the beaten track. Norway is a country whose inhabitants are, not surprisingly, addicted to open-air pursuits, and on cross-country and walking expeditions Rottweilers often act as pack animals, wearing individually fitted pack collars and saddle bags.

The breeding in the 1970s was mostly based on Norwegian dogs with a little influence from Sweden through Swedish, Norwegian and International Champion Fandangos Gyller. There was one kennel, named Hard, which repeated the mating with this dog to a Finnish imported bitch, Inka v. Heidenmoor three times, each litter being a success, with many champions and good working dogs. Some German dogs came in but had little influence.

Today, the Rottweiler is a very popular breed in Norway, and their use for mountain rescue work and police work is increasing.

In Norway Rottweilers are used in rescue work and as sledge dogs.

Sweden

In Sweden the Swedish Kennel Club is the central organisation for all dogs. The Rottweiler breed club (AFR) was founded in 1968 with 58 members and today there are around 650, with registrations running at 400 a year. A magazine is published by the AFR which is one of the most dedicated working breed organisations with very strict recommendations for matings and litters. All dogs to be used for breeding must undergo a mental test, be of good conformation and appearance, be free from hip dysplasia, and must not have been operated on for any inheritable joint defects. All results regarding hip and elbow X-rays, mental tests and other vital information are published twice a year for members. This open policy enables them to follow the development of the breed.

As in most other countries, the Rottweiler is used as a companion and show dog. During the 1970s interest in working competitions increased and today many Rottweilers gain top placings in trials.

The first Rottweiler in Sweden was registered in 1914, but it was not until ten years later that there was organised breeding, which was completely dominated by German imports for many years. However, the influence of Swedish dogs began to be felt during the 1960s. A very successful kennel which had been breeding for some years before this was Lyngsjöns which dominated the breed in the south of Sweden. Another kennel, with the name of Odels, had many beautiful dogs including some German imports. This kennel also exported dogs to Germany.

The 1970s were a time of expansion and a dog, Droll v. St Andreasberg, was imported from Germany. He was used very extensively for breeding, as was his son, Bergsgardens King, a most impressive show dog. Bergsgardens kennel has influenced type to a high degree in Sweden, with many kennels being based on its lines. In order to provide much-needed new blood, Larry v. Stüffelkopf was brought in from Germany and the future will show what contribution he has made to the breed.

Since the 1970s a small portion of the breed has enjoyed great success as working dogs, primarily represented by Fandangos' dogs, now in the ownership of Gunvor af Klinteberg-Järvarud.

Hip dysplasia has been a problem, but to some extent has been kept under control because of the registration and measures for combating it carried out by the Swedish Kennel Club. Also, the insurance companies do not compensate for defective dogs where the parents have the disease. In recent years osteochondrosis of the elbow joint has been an increasing problem, and since 1984 the Rottweiler organisation has received financial support from the Swedish Kennel Club to have as many dogs as possible X-rayed at the elbow. The breeding organisation hopes that in the future breeders will be just as concerned with elbow problems as they are with hip dysplasia.

Denmark

The first Rottweiler came to Denmark in 1911, and since that time numbers have grown steadily with registrations as follows: 1952–115; 1962–237; 1974–640; 1984–835. While registrations have stabilised to between 800 and 900 a year, the membership of the Danish Rottweiler Club has risen over the years to more than 2,500. There is a high degree of participation in the many activities concerned with testing and training puppies as well as adult dogs which are organised by the Club. The Danish Kennel Club registers dogs, not individual breed clubs as in Germany.

In order to be used for breeding, Rottweilers must satisfy two criteria: either they must pass the Mental Test (see page 134), which has a failure rate of 25%, or they must receive a grading of 2 (equivalent to Very Good in Germany) at a show recognised by the Danish Kennel Club. In addition, the hips must be X-rayed with a result of C2 or better on the international scale.

During the last ten to fifteen years, Danish breeders have been trying to move away from the old-fashioned Rottweiler, by which is meant a somewhat heavy, rather lazy and usually a very dominant dog, for which there is really very little use. As well as raising the activity level which is important if you want to train and work with a dog, the degree of dominance has also been lowered as very dominant dogs are not easy to train. Movement has greatly improved and small endurance tests are regularly staged. Here the dogs have to trot next to a bicycle for fifteen kilometres ($9\frac{1}{4}$ miles). This section on gait is also included in the Mental Test when not only is a detailed description of the dog's appearance made, but also the judge studies the dog on the move from a car, so little can escape notice!

Only a small percentage of police dogs are Rottweilers.

Finland

Finland also has a substantial population of Rottweilers with the first being registered with the Finnish Kennel Club in 1938, a bitch called German av Refvelsta. During the last fifteen years some 400 or more Rottweiler puppies have been registered.

Influential imports are: from Sweden, Sonnbos Happy who was in whelp when brought in soon after the Second World War; Blackie, imported by Mr and Mrs Pasanen, who became the foundation bitch for the very famous vom Heidenmoor Kennels; and in 1964 Aviemores Fakir, later to become International and Nordic Champion. Germany produced several animals which played a great part in the

Mr and Mrs
Pasanan's Finnish
Ch. Xantippa v.
Heidenmoor.

development of the breed in Finland: in 1955, Arno vom Martins-
berg, the first to arrive; in 1957, Kao vom Jakobsbrunnen, a very
important dog, Droll vom Wolfsgarten in 1959; Meta v.d. Solitude
and Gerry Eulenspiegel in the early 1970s; and three bitches at the
turn of that decade, the most influential being Jacky v. Hause
Schöttroy through her two sons, Lovenas Lombard in Finland and
Lovenas Lothar in Sweden. Without doubt the most important kennel has been that of Mr and Mrs Pasanen 'vom Heidenmoor' established in 1949. Others include Mr Yrjölä's Juokonheimon kennel, which
produced its first litters in 1950 and after a period of inactivity in the
1960s has now started to breed again; Mrs Roiha's Katajiston kennel;
and Mr Anttonen's Löytövuoren kennel which is well known for its
dual-purpose Rottweilers.

   There are no strict rules or regulations for breeding, but the recommendations given by the Finnish Rottweiler Club are that both parents should be X-rayed and preferably certified free of hip dysplasia,
that both parents should have been shown at least once, and that they
should have passed a character test. The number X-rayed has increased, more so in recent years because the Finnish Club will only
pass on information of those litters where both parents have been
X-rayed, and in 1981 35% of the year's registrations were done.

   Rottweilers have taken part in character or mental tests since 1975.
The test became official on 1 June 1977 and some 50 to 60 dogs are
tested each year; the minimum age is two years.

Further emphasising the Scandinavian breeders' preoccupation with appearance and working capabilities, it is necessary for a Rottweiler to gain one first or two second prizes (grades) in the Working Trials Open Class (medium level), before it can become a Champion.

It is pleasing to learn that the School for the Guide Dogs for the Blind has started to use Rottweilers again in this role and hope to train some more in the future. The breed was used in the 1950s but was dropped from the training programme because of the dog's size and power.

THE MENTAL TEST

This test was devised by the Swedish Working Dog Clubs' Certification Committee and the Breeding Commission in conjunction with the Government Dog School in order that the best possible method of establishing a true picture of the traits tested could be made. It is very different from those normally used and excites some scepticism amongst the uninitiated!

The 12 individual tests are taken in invariant sequence and are designed to ascertain the level of:
- willingness to interact with friendly human beings and dogs,
- inclination to play,
- curiosity – to examine and be aware of its surroundings,
- hunting instinct,
- pack instinct,
- 'fighting' instinct,
- dominance,
- defence instinct,
- gun sureness,
- behaviour appropriate to the situation,
- power of concentration,
- ability to forget unpleasant situations.

From the results of these tests, the dog can receive the training for which it is most suited, e.g. those which are possessed of a pronounced enthusiasm for catching prey should be easy to train for tracking. In this way their behaviour patterns are utilised. The test takes about one hour for each dog and before being tested the dogs are taken for a three mile run (with the handler riding a bicycle) as it has been found that the ability to cope with physical stress is related to dealing with mental stress.

USA

Recollections of visits to the United States bring back memories of the supreme professionalism of the best Rottweiler owners and kennels which is reflected throughout the dog scene over there. At shows, the dogs are presented in top condition and the handlers are never less than immaculate, showing the dogs with total expertise – possibly achieving the highest standard of showmanship anywhere.

The same degree of professionalism applies to the best dog trainers and their methods, with scientific principles being fully utilised to enable training to proceed with speed and efficiency. The trainers, Jack and Wendy Volhard, Gail Fisher and the Canadian, Glen Johnson, deserve the highest praise. All of them have given lectures and courses in this country and all have written useful books.

A notable German import, American Ch. Dux v. Hungerbuhl. (Rodsden's Rottweilers and Dr Eken).

Rottweilers have been established for more than half a century in the USA, the first litter being whelped in 1930, bred by a German immigrant who had been an established breeder in his own country. Although this litter was born in the USA, it was recorded in the German Stud Book. 1931 saw the first Rottweiler admitted to the American Kennel Club Stud Book – Stina v. Felsenmeer – and her litter born the same year was the first to be registered in the AKC. Two other breeders, also from Germany, bred litters during the 1930s which were also registered in the German Stud Book.

Today, the breed is undergoing a tremendous boom in the USA, with all which that implies, and large numbers of dogs are imported from abroad, mainly from Germany, Holland and Scandinavia. It is said that too many of the best specimens cross the Atlantic to the detriment of the breed's future in the countries concerned, but only time will tell.

Some really outstanding dogs have been imported: Bundessieger Harras v. Sofienbusch SchH1, his son Bundessieger Erno v. Wellesweiler SchH1 (American Champion) Dux v. Hungerbuhl SchH1, all from Germany and all top producers. More recently several very good dogs have come in from Holland, notably Oscar and Quanto v.h. Brabantpark. It is, perhaps, a source of some envy to us here that there is no period of quarantine for imported dogs, as it certainly makes it a less expensive procedure and easier on the dogs. But this reasoning is insignificant next to the importance of keeping rabies out of the UK.

Many fine dogs have been bred in the States, and there are certainly enough lines available to keep breeding going in a stable direction for decades, but it is something of a status symbol to have an imported dog. Interestingly, matings between closely related dogs are not carried out by the leading breeders; outcrossing seems to be the preferred method. The main reason advanced for this is that experience indicates that there is an increased risk of unsoundness in line or inbreeding.

Not unexpectedly, there are many Rottweiler Breed Clubs, the longest established ones being Colonial, Medallion, Golden State and Western Rottweiler Owners. Several have a Code of Ethics (a code of conduct for members as breeders and owners) violations of which are treated very seriously, and advertisements for litters for sale are not accepted for publication in club magazines unless both parents have been X-rayed for hip dysplasia and declared normal by the certifying authority, the Orthopaedic Foundation for Animals.

Many Rottweilers are trained and worked in obedience trials. The exercises are somewhat easier than those in UK trials but this in no way detracts from the US owners' achievements for the dogs *have* to be trained to a very good standard in order to compete. There is also more interest in the working side in the States.

Dog shows are very popular and are regarded as a day out by exhibitors and spectators alike. Champions are made up according to a points system and generally dogs are entered in one class only, with a separate class for champions so that up-and-coming young dogs do not have to come into competition with them for the points. The number of points depends on how many dogs are entered in each breed.

It is by no means an uncommon occurrence for dogs to go on a show circuit with professional handlers to try to obtain multiple show honours. They can also be 'leased' to other breeders for periods of time. These are indicative of a 'stockbreeder's' attitude and cannot be without stress for the dogs. This type of behaviour is, I think, open to question.

American Ch.
Powderhorn's Lars
of Wencrest.

13   The Essential Rottweiler

Rottweilers along with other working breeds like German Shepherd Dogs, Boxers and Dobermanns have been the object of carefully controlled breeding in their country of origin designed to perpetuate all that is best in physical and mental qualities. All these breeds have suffered from excessive popularity and indiscriminate breeding has taken place, so in this book I have emphasised three main points.

1. The absolute necessity of paying scrupulous attention to breeding only from sound and typical dogs and bitches in a ceaseless endeavour to produce sturdy, healthy, handsome puppies.

2. The need for potential owners of large and strong guard breeds like the Rottweiler to have the personality and the facilities to ensure a happy human–dog partnership.

3. The requirement for socialisation and training of the Rottweiler in order to fit him for our modern world.

Nowadays, there is much less tolerance in England towards the dog, with more and more restrictions being placed upon owners. The anti-dog lobby is perfectly entitled to its opinions and all of us who care deeply about our Rottweilers should do our utmost to ensure they are not disturbers of the peace, scavengers, sources of infection or 'latch-key' animals. Above all, the breed is not one which should be allowed to roam or go out unsupervised.

Twenty-five years of Rottweiler ownership have given me deep pleasure and acquaintance with many dogs and bitches which have been integral members of the family; adaptable, loyal and affectionate, go-anywhere, do-anything dogs.

The tremendous versatility of the Rottweiler is one of its most endearing features: the best of companions and guards by any standard; impressive in appearance; a first rate worker; extremely agile; and highly intelligent with an excellent nose for tracking and searching.

Despite his size, a Rottweiler fits very well into the domestic scene: he is peaceful in the home; he barks only when there is good reason to do so; and, having a docked tail, coffee cups and the like are not swept off low tables! They accompany babies in prams, supervise toddlers, announce the arrival of strangers and are always cheerful and welcoming, a marvellous comfort when one is feeling in low spirits. A big friendly black face and wagging stump of a tail can do marvels for the morale!

To the dog owner, a walk without one's dog is unthinkable and car trips with no big black nose giving the occasional reassuring nudge on the shoulder are lonely affairs.

Many Rottweilers are great swimmers, while some remain 'paddlers', taking in great gulps of water. Others, living the rural life, accompany their owners when they go riding and can readily be trained to heel to the horse on and off the lead.

Rottweilers are extremely responsive and affectionate towards members of the household, and can fairly be described as family dogs rather than one-man dogs. They are fun-loving and greatly enjoy games, but they have an innate sense of dignity, the males especially dislike over-familiarity from strangers.

The more you involve your Rottweiler in your life, the better a companion he will make. Adaptable and able to meet all situations with composure and confidence, he makes the ideal partner for the discerning, capable and caring owner.

Rottweilers are adaptable. Mr Matterson's Francesca from Blackforest.

Companions. Mr G.
Mabbutt's Nobane
Cranleigh is an
adored pet.

Mrs A. ten Bruggencate's Caro v.d. Horstlinde. The shape of things to come?

Mrs Grunerwald's Ch. Cache v. Grunerwald taking his daily swim.

Appendix 1

Further Reading

BREED BOOKS

Der Rottweiler, translation, Hans Korn 1939, pub. Colonel Rottweiler Club, USA.

Studies in the Breed History of the Rottweiler, translation, Manfred Schanzle, 1967, pub. Colonel and Medallion Rottweiler Clubs, USA.

Know your Rottweiler, translation, D. Chardet, 1977, pub. Powderhorn Press, USA.

The Complete Rottweiler, Muriel Freeman, 1984, pub. Howell Book House, USA.

TRAINING

Training Your Dog, The Step by Step Manual, Volhard and Fisher, 1984, pub. Howell Book House, USA.

Tracking Dog, Theory and Methods, Glen Johnson, 1977, pub. Arner Publications, USA.

VETERINARY

First Aid for Pets, R.W. Kirk, 1978, Sunrise Book, pub. Dutton, USA.

Dog Breeding, Kay White, 1980, pub. Bartholomew & Son.

Dog and Cat Nutrition, ed. A.T.B. Edney, 1982, pub. Pergamon Press.

GENERAL

Understanding your Dog, M.W. Fox, 1972, pub. Blond and Briggs.

The Natural History of the Dog, R. and A. Fiennes, 1968, pub. Weidenfeld and Nicolson.

Your Dog and the Law, G. Sandys Winch, 1984, pub. Shaw & Sons.

Appendix 2

Addresses
The Kennel Club, 1 Clarges Street, Piccadilly, London W1.

BREED CLUBS
The Rottweiler Club
British Rottweiler Association
Midland Rottweiler Club
Northern Rottweiler Club   As Breed Club Secretaries change,
Scottish Rottweiler Club   the names and addresses of the cur-
Welsh Rottweiler Club   rent holders of this office may be
Northern Ireland Rottweiler   obtained from the Kennel Club.
Club

WEEKLY DOG PUBLICATIONS
Dog World, Clergy House, The Churchyard, Ashford, Kent.
Our Dogs, 5 Oxford Road, Station Approach, Manchester M60 1SX.
Dog Training Weekly, 7 Greenwich South Street, London SE10 8BR.

INSURANCE COMPANIES
Pet Plan, 319 Chiswick High Road, London W4.
Dog Breeders Insurance Co Ltd, 12 Christchurch Road, Bourne-
mouth, Dorset.

Appendix 3

THE ROTTWEILER STANDARD
No. 147b   F C I   March 25, 1970

The Breed Characteristics of the Rottweiler:

I. General Appearance

   Rottweiler breeding aims at a powerful dog, black with well-defined mahogany markings, which despite a massive general appearance is not lacking in nobility, and is particularly suitable as a companion, guard and working dog.

The Rottweiler is a robust dog, rather above medium size, neither clumsy nor light, neither tall on the leg nor like a Greyhound. His frame, which is compact, strong and well-proportioned, gives every indication of great strength, agility and endurance. His appearance gives an immediate impression of determination and courage; his demeanour is self-assured, steady and fearless. His calm gaze indicates good humour.

He reacts with great alertness to his surroundings and to his master.

Size: Height at withers:

Dogs 60–68 cm	Bitches 55–63 cm
60–61 small	55–57 small
62–64 medium	58–59 medium
65–66 large	60–61 large
67–68 very large	62–63 very large

The measurement for the length of the trunk, measured from the breast bone to the point of rump, should not exceed the height at the withers by more than 15%.

II. Head

   Of medium length, broad between the ears, the forehead line, seen in profile, moderately arched. The occipital bone is well developed, without protruding too much. The stop and zygomatic arch are well pronounced. The relations of the head are 40% of the total length between bridge of nose and inner eye angle, 60% from inner eye angle to occipital bone.

Scalp: Tightly drawn all over, only forming slight wrinkle when the dog is extremely alert. The aim is a head without wrinkles.

Lips: Black, lying close, corners of the mouth closed.

Nose: The bridge of the nose is straight, broad at the root and moderately tapering. Tip of the nose well developed, broad rather than round, with relatively large nostrils and always black in colour.

Eyes: Medium size, almond-shaped and dark brown in colour, with well-fitting eyelids.

Ears: As small as possible, pendant, triangular, set well apart and high. When the ears are well placed and laid forward, the skull appears broader.

Teeth: Strong and complete (42 teeth). The upper incisors closing scissors-like over those of the lower jaw.

III. Neck
Powerful, moderately long, well-muscled, with a slightly arched line rising from the shoulders; dry, without dewlap or loose skin on the throat.

IV. Trunk
Roomy, broad and deep chest, with a well-developed forechest and well-sprung ribs. Back straight, powerful and firm. Loins short, powerful and deep. Flanks not drawn up. Croup broad, of medium length and slightly rounded, neither straight nor too sloping.

V. Tail
Carried horizontally, short and strong. Must be docked if too long at birth.

VI. Forequarters
Shoulders long and well set. The upper arm lies well against the body, but not too tightly. Lower arm strongly developed and muscular. Pasterns slightly springy, strong, not steep. Feet round, very compact and arched. Pads hard, nails short, black and strong.
The forelegs, seen from the front, are straight and not set too close together. The lower arms, seen from the side, are straight.
The shoulders should have a lay-back of about 45°; the angle between the shoulder blade and the upper arm is about 115°.

VII. Hindquarters

Upper thigh fairly long, broad and well muscled. Lower thigh long, powerful, sinewy, broadly muscled, leading to a powerful hock, well angulated, not steep.

The back feet are somewhat longer than the front feet, equally compact and arched, with strong toes and without dewclaws.

Seen from behind, the back legs are straight and not set too close. In a natural stance, the upper thigh and hipbone, upper thigh and lower thigh, and lower thigh and metatarsus form obtuse angles. The slope of the hipbone is about 20°–30°.

VIII. Movement

The Rottweiler is a trotter. In this gait, he conveys the impression of strength, endurance and determination. The back stays firm and relatively still. The motion is harmonious, steady, powerful and unhindered with a good length of stride.

IX. Coat

Consists of outer coat and undercoat. The former is bristly, of medium length, coarse, dense and lying close. The undercoat must not show through the outer coat. The hair is somewhat longer on both front and hind legs.

The colour is black with well-defined markings of a rich, red-brown colour on the cheeks, muzzle, throat, chest and legs, as well as over the eyes and under the tail.

X. Character

The character of the Rottweiler consists of the sum of all the inherited and acquired physical and mental attributes, qualities and abilities, which determine and regulate his behaviour toward his surroundings.

With regard to his mental make-up, his disposition is basically friendly and peaceful; he is faithful, obedient and willing to work. His temperament, his drive for action and for moving about are moderate. His reaction to disagreeable stimuli is tough, fearless and assured.

His senses are appropriately developed. His reactions are quick and his learning capacity is excellent. He is a strong, well-balanced type of dog. Because of his unsuspicious nature, moderate sharpness and high self-confidence, he reacts quietly and without haste to his surroundings. When threatened, however, he goes into action immediately because of his highly developed fighting and protection instincts. Faced with painful experiences, he holds his ground, fearless and unflinching. When the threat passes, his fighting mood subsides relatively quickly and changes to a peaceful one.

Among his other good qualities are: A strong attachment to his home and a constant readiness to defend it; he is very willing to retrieve and has a good capacity for tracking; he has considerable endurance, likes the water, and is fond of children. He does not have a well-developed hunting instinct.

In more detail, the following instincts and character attributes are considered desirable:

a) In daily life	Self-confidence	High
	Fearlessness	High
	Temperament	Medium
	Endurance	High
	Mobility and Activity	Medium
	Alertness	High
	Tractability	Medium-High
	Mistrust	Low-Medium
	Sharpness	Low-Medium
b) As companion, guard and working dog	all the qualities named under a) as well as:	
	Courage	Very High
	Fighting instinct	Very High
	Protection Instinct	Very High
	Hardness	High
c) Guarding characteristics	Watchfulness	Medium
	Threshold of Excitability	Medium
d) Aptitude for nose work	Searching Instinct	Medium
	Tracking Instinct	High
	Willingness to Retrieve	Medium-High

It should be noted that these instincts and qualities may be present in varying degrees of intensity, and that they often merge into one another and are interrelated. They must, however, be present and as highly developed as is necessary for working efficiency.

XI. Appearance and Working Faults

Appearance faults are noticeable deviations from the features described in the Standard. They lessen the working value of the dog only to a limited degree, but they can obscure and distort the typical image of the breed. Appearance faults, according to the breed Standard, include the following:

Light, tall, Greyhound-like in general appearance; too long, too short, narrow body; prominent occipital bone; hound-like head and expression; narrow, light, too short, too long, or coarse head; flat forehead (little or no stop); narrow lower jaw; long or pointed muzzle; cheeks too protruding; ram's or split nose, bridge of nose dished or sloping; tip of nose light or spotted; open, pink or spotted lips, corners of the mouth open; distemper teeth; wrinkles on the head; ears set too low, large, long, floppy, turned back, not lying close, or irregularly carried; light (yellow) eyes, or a light and a dark eye, open, deep-set, too full, round, staring eyes, piercing gaze; neck too long, thick, weak-muscled, dewlaps or loose skin on throat; forelegs set narrow or not straight; light nail's; tail set too high or too low; coat soft, too short or too long, wavy coat, absence of undercoat; markings of the wrong colour, poorly defined or too extensive; white spots; dewclaws on the hindlegs.

More serious than the faults mentioned above are those deviations from the ideal which affect both the appearance of the dog and its working qualities. They are called working faults and are listed in the Standard as follows:

Weak bones and musculature; steep shoulders, deficient elbow articulation; too long, too short, or steep upper arm; weak or steep pasterns; splay feet; flat feet or excessively arched toes, stunted toes; flat ribcage, barrel chest, pigeon breast; back too long, weak, sway or roach; croup too short, too straight, too long or too steep; too heavy, unwieldy body; hindlegs flatshanked, sickle-hocked, cow-hocked or bow-legged; joints too narrowly or too widely angled.

Excluded from judging and breeding are:
1. Dogs lacking one or both testicles. Both testicles must be well-developed and clearly visible in the scrotum.
2. All Rottweilers showing an abnormality in the hip joint. The degree of abnormality leading to disqualification, and the measures to be taken by breeders, are set forth by the Breeding Committee.
3. All Rottweilers with faulty bites and dentition; i.e. over-shot, under-shot and missing premolars or molars (X-rays are not accepted as proof of complete dentition).
4. All Rottweilers with loose or rolled-in eyelids (entropion) as well as those with open eyelids (ectropion). In case of doubt, veterinary examination is recommended when a dog with eye trouble is presented at a breed show or breeding eligibility test. The judge is responsible for sending information about the dog in question

to the Studbook Office. If the trouble is still present when the dog is shown again, or if the eyelids have been operated on, the dog is forever banned from breeding. Concealment of an eye operation is one of the worst deceptions, and according to the show rules is to be prosecuted as a breeding violation.

5. All Rottweilers with yellow eyes, hawk eyes, staring expression or with eyes of different colours.
6. All Rottweilers with pronounced reversal of sexual characteristics (bitchy dogs, doggy bitches).
7. All timid, cowardly, gunshy, vicious, excessively mistrustful and nervous Rottweilers, as well as those of stupid expression and behaviour. Dogs which show obvious laziness, unusually slow re-actions or extreme one-sidedness in their character should be watched and examined with particular care before they are used for breeding (the possibility of deafness should be considered).
8. Decidedly long-coated or wavy-coated Rottweilers. Smooth-coated or short-coated dogs with an absence of undercoat should be used for breeding only with the permission of the chief breed warden.

The teeth: The adult dog has 42 teeth; 12 incisors, 4 fangs or corner teeth, 16 premolars and 10 molars. The teeth are of extremely vital importance to the dog. No Rottweiler will be judged or used for breeding who does not have a well-formed, correct and complete set of teeth.

With very few exceptions, depending on the shape of the dog's head, all should have the so-called 'scissors-bite'. It is the natural, regular set of teeth, which all dogs have, whereby the upper incisors seize – slightly grinding – a little bit over the lower ones. If this grinding touch is missing, there will be a clear space between the incisors of the upper jaw and those of the lower jaw. This is called an overbite. If the teeth of the lower jaw are in front of those of the upper jaw, one considers it an underbite. Both forms are defects and result in disqualification of the dog. A set of teeth like pincers, biting upon one another; i.e., both rows of the incisors touching each other directly, is still admissible. However, it usually degrades the dog and puts him one class lower when he is judged.

Running Gear and Gaits: The hindquarters are the means of support and act as a leverage for locomotion. In every type of action the forward thrust proceeds from the hindquarters, which are more strongly angulated and have more powerful and complex muscles than the forequarters. In conformity with the greater strain placed on them, the forequarters show a less angled system for support and braking. The propulsive forces are transmitted to the forequarters through the trunk. The back plays an essential part in the forward movement, the powerful extensor muscles of the neck and back cooperating with the lower neck muscles, as well as with those of the inside thigh and stomach. Extremely strong and well-developed back muscles are essential for a good and enduring gait.

The types of gait in the Rottweiler are the walk, the trot, the pace, the gallop and the leap.

In the trot, the forequarters and hindquarters are mutually synchronised (brace, lift, float, support). The back remains relatively stable.

In the walk, the back movements are more visible; in the pace (simultaneous advance of the hind and front limbs on one side), they are more pronounced, and strongest of all in the gallop, when the back is arched like a spring and throws the body forward.

Faulty types of gait are: Stiff, constrained, too high or dragging the ground, short steps, rocking, swaying, rolling, weaving.

General Comments on External Appearance: Defects in harmony (balance) and soundness of the body structure detract from the dog's appearance and working ability.

A dog's working usefulness depends essentially on his ability to move and run, and these factors, therefore, receive particular attention in assessing the appearance and character. There are several references in the Standard to the importance of the length and power of the limbs, the back and shoulders, the angulation of the joints and the muscles.

In judging a living thing, other imponderables also come into play, which only the trained eye of an experienced judge can correctly assess within the framework of the total picture.

A few figures may be mentioned for guidance: A Rottweiler, which is 65 cm at the withers, should measure about 75 cm from the breast bone to the point of rump. The chest circumference should be about equal to the height at the withers plus 20 cm. The chest depth should be neither more, nor very much less, than 50% of the height at the withers.

Appendix 4

Conditions of Sale Agreement
                    (As recommended by the Rottweiler Club)
The Vendor .... of .... warrants
title to the animal but no other warranty as to soundness or otherwise
is given except as may be implied by law. The vendor has endea-
voured by breeding practice to reduce the risk that the unsoundness
of the animal may in the future be seriously affected by an inherited
defect, e.g. hip dysplasia, which is not present at the time of sale.
Such risk shall be borne by the purchaser provided that:

(a) If a veterinary surgeon shall within .... months of delivery of
the animal certify that the soundness of the animal is seriously
affected by an inherited defect, then the vendor shall refund to the
purchaser .... per cent of the purchase price.

(b) If a veterinary surgeon shall more than .... months but less
than ..... months after delivery so certify, then the vendor shall
refund to the purchaser such percentage of the purchase price (not
exceeding ..... per cent) as may in the circumstances be agreed as
reasonable, or in default of agreement, as may be determined by an
arbitrator to be nominated by the President for the time being of the
Rottweiler Club.

The purchaser has read and accepts the above conditions of Sale.

Dated this ..... day of ..... 19... Signed: .....

N.B. This agreement is reproduced by kind permission of the Rottweiler Club.

Appendix 5

The Rottweiler Code of Ethics

1. a. I agree to co-operate and participate with the Rottweiler Club of Great Britain and other show-giving Clubs to share aid and information with those interested in the breed, and to encourage and exhibit sportsmanlike conduct in all competitions.
   b. I agree to read and familiarise myself with the Kennel Club standard for the Rottweiler.

2. BREEDING
   a. I will only breed from those dogs and bitches believed to be clear from known serious hereditary defects and which are mentally stable and not suffering from acute nervous problems.
   b. I will keep accurate records of breedings, sales and registrations. I will at all times be extremely cautious when advertising or selling as to a true and realistic description of stock, especially as to potential prospects of young stock, in case it should inadvertently be implying guaranteed show success.
   c. I will breed from healthy, mature dogs and bitches, conscientiously planning each litter. Bitches would not be used for breeding prior to two years of age and not be bred from more frequently than alternate seasons and not be used for breeding after the age of seven years, a stud dog owner to satisfy him- or herself as to the suitability of the bitch's breeding and the conditions under which the litter would be reared.

3. SALE OF ROTTWEILERS
   a. I will attempt to help buyers and be available to answer questions and provide assistance.
   b. I will only sell puppies that are to the best of my knowledge in good health and exhibit sound temperament and are at least seven weeks old, and will provide with the pedigree at the time of sale a satisfactory diet sheet, complete health record and details of worming. Any puppies sold over the age of twelve weeks would be fully inoculated.

c. I shall not knowingly sell Rottweilers to commercial wholesale dealers, retailers or laboratories, nor allow my stock to become raffle or competition prizes, and shall exercise every possible care as to the suitability of my Rottweilers' future homes.

d. I shall provide Kennel Club registration or application for each puppy sold and at least a three-generation pedigree. If registration is to be withheld, it must be by mutual agreement in writing.

4. I will remember that my prime concern as a breeder is to produce healthy, sound dogs that will be a credit to the breed. I will be honest in dealings with buyers and fellow-breeders and will endeavour to co-operate towards a programme of improvement for the breed. When a puppy (or puppies) is taken in lieu of a stud fee or as part of breeding terms, I understand that the vendor is fully responsible for the condition of the puppy (puppies), and that their puppy (puppies) should not be sold unseen. I understand that breeding terms must not be used as a means of foisting stock on to those persons unable to afford the price of a puppy, and such agreements should only be used to place bitches in homes where their welfare and furtherance of the breed have been fully investigated. (A legal breeding terms contract should then be drawn up.)

I will at all times maintain a high standard of health and care for the Rottweiler and will not deliberately libel or slander another person or make vicious comments on another's stock.

Reproduced by kind permission of the Rottweiler Club.

Appendix 6

Hip Dysplasia – International Certificate
The Federation Cynologique Internationale instituted an international certificate of the hip dysplasia status of X-rayed dogs in 1983. Each country has its own scheme with various descriptions of the results; for example, there being five grades in Germany, seven in Holland etc. The International Certificate has five grades, A–E, each being divided into 1 and 2 and there are therefore ten possible classifications. C1/C2 are classified as mild H.D.

There is no direct comparison with the BVA/KC HD Scoring Scheme in which dogs in England are given a score of from 0–106 maximum, making a possible 107 grades of severity. Mr D. G. Clayton-Jones MRCVS DVR of the Royal Veterinary College, London, a scrutineer for the BVA Scheme, in a private communication has given an unofficial estimate of the comparison with the International Certificate:

0–4 is approximately equal to A1/2 (old BVA Certificate)

4–12 is approximately equal to B1/2 (approx. old BVA Breeder's Letter)

The United Kingdom is not a member of the FCI but since many pedigrees of dogs here contain names of imported dogs with a description of their hip status, a table of the various grades of hip status in five FCI countries is given below.

First-aid Kit
Scissors (with rounded ends)
Bandages – open weave gauze, 1″ and 2″ rolls (1 each)
Bandage, crepe 2″ (1)
Roll of adhesive tape
Roll of cotton wool
Gamgee – antiseptic gauze dressing pads
Rectal thermometer (1)
Small carton of cotton buds
Pair cut-off tights for preventing ear-shaking (emergency use)
Hydrogen peroxide
Kaolin mixture
Aureomycin eye ointment
Betsolan cream (grazes, burns, stings, sore feet)

Classification, Einstufung	Classification, Klassifizierung	SF Finland Finnland	NL The Netherlands Niederlande	D Germany Deutschland	S Sweden Schweden	CH Switzerland Schweiz	Classification, Einstufung
1	No signs of hip dysplasia	Ei-dysplasiaa "hyvät"	Negatief geheel gaaf (1)	Kein Hinweis für HD	Utmärkt	Frei	1
A					U.A		A
2	Kein Hinweis für HD	Ei-dysplasiaa	Negatief niet geheel gaaf (2)				2
1	Transitional Case Übergangsform (verdächtig für HD)	Rajata-paus	Transitional case (Tc)	Übergangs form (verdächtig für HD)			1
B							B
2							2
1	Mild	I	Licht positief (3)	Leichte HD	I	I	1
C							C
2	Leichte HD						2
1	Moderate Mittlere HD	I	Positief (3½)	Mittlere HD	II	II	1
D							D
2			Positief (4)				2
1	Severe	III		Schwere HD	III	III	1
E							E
2	Schwere HD		Positief optima forma (5)			IV	2

Appendix 7

Litter Weights
Blackforest 'H' Litter-s. Rintelna The Bombardier CDex, UDex, d. Anouk from Blackforest. Breeder Mrs M. Macphail

	Week 1	Week 2	Week 3	Week 4	Week 5	Week 6	Week 7	Week 8
DOGS								
Green	1·12	2·14	4·8	6·8	9·0	11·0	14·0	16·0
Yellow	1·9	2·12	3·13	6·2	8·2	10·4	11·0	14·0
BITCHES								
Blue	1·9	2·9	2·12	5·8	7·6	9·8	12·0	—
Brown	1·11	2·9	3·12	5·6	7·8	9·6	12·0	—
White	1·9	2·10	4·0	5·14	8·0	9·12	12·0	—
Navy*	1·9	2·8	3·11	5·14	7·12	7·12	8·0	—
Red	1·9	2·10	4·2	5·12	7·8	9·12	12·0	14·0
Tan	1·13	3·0	3·12	5·10	7·8	9·12	12·0	—

Notes: 1. *This puppy was ill with an unidentified virus problem, hence the cessation of weight gain for one week, but she eventually caught up with the others.
2. The colours refer to the collars worn for identification purposes.

'Madason' Litter, breeder Mrs M. Atkinson. s. Ch. Prince Gelert of Bhaluk. d. Blackforest Madame Melite.

	Day 1	Day 3	Day 4	Day 5	Day 6	Day 7	Weight Gain	Day 8	Day 9	Day 10	Day 11	Day 12	Day 13	Day 14
Bitch														
6·30 1	13oz	14oz	15oz	1·1oz	1·3½	1·5	8oz	1·6	1·7½	1·10½	1·11	1·15	2·00	2·1½
8·45 6	13oz	15oz	1·1	1·2½	1·4½	1·6½	9½oz	1·7½	1·11	1·12½	1·14½	2·1	2·3	2·5½
8·50 7	13oz	16oz	1·2	1·3½	1·5	1·7	10oz	1·8½	1·2	1·4	2·00	2·1½	2·3½	2·5½
10·00 9	9oz	10oz	12oz	13½oz	15oz	1·1½	8½oz	1·2½	1·5	1·6½	1·9	1·10	1·12	1·13½
Dog														
7·05 2	14oz	16oz	1·4½	1·6	1·8	1·10	12oz	1·12	1·14	2·0	2·2	2·4	2·6	2·9
8·05 3	12oz	1·2	1·5	1·6	1·8	1·11	15oz	1·12	1·14	1·15	2·2	2·3½	2·5	2·8
8·20 4	12oz	14½oz	1·2	1·3½	1·6	1·7	1·7½	1·10½	1·12	1·14½	1·15	2·1	2·3	
8·25 5	12oz	13oz	14oz	1·1	1·3	1·4	8oz	1·6	1·7	1·10	1·11	1·12	1·14	1·15
9·00 8	14oz	1·1	1·2	1·2½	1·6	1·9	11oz	1·10	1·11½	1·13	1·15	2·0	2·3	2·5
10·15 10	1·0	1·4	1·6	1·8	1·11½	1·14	14oz	2·0	2·3	2·4	2·8	2·8	2·11	2·13

Note: timings are birth times.

The weights given in the tables above are not meant to be the ideals at different ages from birth but merely to give ideas of the type of records to keep and gains made from day to day and week to week, an essential way of monitoring development.

Index

Index to Dog Names